"What about the baby?" Oliver asked. "We just can't leave her here."

"Dr. Shepherd wants to check her over at the hospital," Ella explained.

"But I thought you were the baby doctor?"

"I am, sweetie, but Sheriff Hank figured I'd probably want to spend time with my own babies tonight."

"I'm not a baby," Oliver pointed out.

"I am," Owen said. "I'm never running away— Hey, look! There's Dillon's mom. And she's crying and hugging his dad. They getting married again?"

The polite thing would have been to grant them some privacy. So how come Ella couldn't tear her eyes away from the sight of Jackson with his ex?

Dear Reader,

As an eighties teen, one of my fave movies was *Three Men and a Baby*—and of course the sequel! The concept of those three hunky, accomplished men falling to pieces while caring for that sweet little baby always makes me smile. Which is why, after seeing a late-night running of the film, I couldn't help but wonder what would happen if three equally adorable little boys were to find themselves in a similar situation. Being kids, of course, their parents would have to be brought into the situation, and naturally, mayhem ensues!

Even before having a newborn thrust into their lives, Ella and Jackson both have plenty of personal issues to work through. Longtime acquaintances, the two find it all too easy to fall for each other over baby bathing and feedings. Trouble is, seeing how Jackson's son has his heart set on a reunion between his recently divorced parents, this hunky fireman has no business falling for a pretty pediatrician!

Happy reading!

Laura Marie

Three Boys and a Baby

LAURA MARIE ALTOM

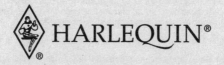

HARLEQUIN®

TORONTO • NEW YORK • LONDON
AMSTERDAM • PARIS • SYDNEY • HAMBURG
STOCKHOLM • ATHENS • TOKYO • MILAN • MADRID
PRAGUE • WARSAW • BUDAPEST • AUCKLAND

ISBN-13: 978-0-373-75215-7
ISBN-10:   0-373-75215-6

THREE BOYS AND A BABY

Copyright © 2008 by Laura Marie Altom.

This edition published by arrangement with Harlequin Books S.A.

® and TM are trademarks of the publisher. Trademarks indicated with ® are registered in the United States Patent and Trademark Office, the Canadian Trade Marks Office and in other countries.

www.eHarlequin.com

Printed in U.S.A.

ABOUT THE AUTHOR

After college (Go Hogs!), bestselling, award-winning author Laura Marie Altom did a brief stint as an interior designer before becoming a stay-at-home mom to boy/girl twins. Always an avid romance reader, she knew it was time to try her hand at writing when she found herself replotting the afternoon soaps.

When not immersed in her next story, Laura enjoys an almost glamorous lifestyle of zipping around in a convertible while trying to keep her dog from leaping out, and constantly striving to reach the bottom of the laundry basket—a feat she may never accomplish! For real fun, Laura is content to read, do needlepoint and cuddle with her kids and handsome hubby.

Laura loves hearing from readers at either P.O. Box 2074, Tulsa, OK 74101, or e-mail: BaliPalm@aol.com. Love lounging on the beach while winning fun stuff? Check out lauramariealtom.com!

Books by Laura Marie Altom

HARLEQUIN AMERICAN ROMANCE

*U.S. Marshals

For my new friend and partner in miscellaneous mischief, Melinda Taylor. You're a hoot!

Chapter One

"Cool! Can we keep it?"

Oliver Garvey, a full minute older than his identical eight-year-old twin, Owen, peeked into the basket and fell in love. The baby was a girl. He knew, because her blanket was pink. So were her pajamas, but the note that was safety-pinned to them was written on yellow paper. It read: Please take care of me. Since Oliver was oldest, and therefore smartest, he said, "Duh. Of course we're gonna keep it. What kind of dummy are you?"

"Don't call me a dummy," Owen said, almost falling off the neighborhood park's merry-go-round while making a fist. "*You're* a dummy."

"Can I name her?" their seven-year-old neighbor and friend, Dillon Tate, asked. "I always wanted a baby, but Dad says they're loud and smelly."

"She doesn't seem loud or smelly to me," Owen said.

"Just wait till she poops." Oliver sniffed the part of her blanket where the stinky stuff would be. "I saw in a movie one time where babies poop a lot. We're going to have to find some diapers."

"I bet Mom has some," Owen suggested. "We'll tell her to bring 'em home from the clinic." Their mother was a kid doctor, so she always had kid gear around in case of an emergency. Lots of times they'd seen her do medicine stuff, so Owen was pretty much a doctor himself.

"No!" Dillon crossed his arms and stomped his right foot. "I don't wanna tell your mom."

"What's wrong with you?" Oliver asked him.

"You guys, that's what. You can't go calling your mom at a time like this."

"Why come?" Owen wanted to know.

"'Cause this is a *boys only* club. Why do you want to make your mom a member?"

"We don't," Oliver said, "but she knows all about babies. She's a doctor."

"My dad knows about babies, too. He's a fireman. Plus, he's a guy, which makes him a lot better to be with than your mom."

"I love Mom," Owen said. "She's a good cook."

"I didn't say she wasn't." Dillon rolled his eyes. "All I meant was that this is a guy club and we need to keep the baby a guy secret."

"What do you think?" Owen asked, turning to his older brother.

Oliver took a moment to consider the facts. He guessed his mom probably knew more about babies, but she *was* a girl. Dillon's dad knew lots about fires and stuff, though, so if the baby caught on fire, he'd know what to do. Of course, they could just ask the baby who she wanted to go to, but that would be kind of stupid since she didn't even know how to talk. In case the other guys laughed at him, Oliver kept that last idea to himself.

"Well?" Owen and Dillon asked.

"I agree with Dillon. We need to keep this a guy secret."

"Shouldn't we vote?" Owen asked.

Oliver sighed. "Raise your hand if you think we should take it to Dillon's dad."

Oliver and Dillon raised their hands.

"Okay," Oliver said, "now raise your hand if you want to take it to our mom."

Owen and Dillon raised their hands.

"You can't vote twice, Dillon." Honestly, at the moment, Oliver was kind of mad with his best friend. "Which do you want?"

"I want my dad, but I didn't want Owen to feel bad. Plus, your mom *is* a good cook."

Oliver sighed. Geez Louise, it was hard work being around such lamebrains. "Okay, let's vote again. Who wants Dillon's dad?"

Oliver and Dillon raised their hands.

"Our mom?"

Owen and the baby raised their hands.

"Oh, come on," Oliver said. "Owen, get away from the baby. You're gonna break its arm."

"Am not."

"Are, too."

"That's it," Oliver said. "I'm the boss of both of you, and I say we're takin' it to Dillon's dad."

Owen stuck out his tongue.

IT WAS DONE.

Her baby would be all right. From watching all three boys at one time or another at the neighborhood day care, she knew they came from wonderful, loving homes. The kind of home she'd never be able to provide for her precious baby girl.

Giving her up had been the hardest thing she'd ever done. Harder than running away for seven months, then living in that group home for pregnant teens so that her grandma and father would never feel the shame.

Giving away her baby had been even harder than taking her from the group home's nursery, then hitching her way back to her miniscule hometown of Brown, Kansas—renamed during the 1930s when there'd been a drought. Before that, the town had been called Garden Glade. Her Sunday-school teacher had said that every so often some outraged garden-club member circulated a petition to change the name back to the original, but so far, Brown had stuck.

Hearing her baby cry, and not being able to go to her, she figured the name suited this place just fine.

Brown.

Not really black, but its depressing neighbor.

JACKSON TATE had had a bad day, and judging by the squalling coming from inside his house, it was about to get worse.

Feet leaden as he crossed the wood-planked front porch, he yanked open the screen door, growling when it fell off the top hinge. Great. Just one more thing needing to be fixed.

Back before his ex had left, he'd taken pride in keeping up the old place. Julie had been the one who'd wanted to sink their meager savings into the nineteenth-century money pit. She'd said the Victorian home and the neighborhood that was as old as the State would not only be a good investment, but with its proximity to schools and the oak-lined park it would be the perfect place to raise a family.

Right. Only, *what* family, seeing as how she'd deemed her law career more interesting than either her husband or son.

After kicking off his regulation shoes, he unbuttoned his blue uniform shirt.

Dammit. Why couldn't he get through a single, freakin' day

without letting her leaving get to him? He didn't still have a thing for her. Best as he could tell, he just missed the way things used to be. The way the house had felt more like a home.

"Dad, Dad!" His son, Dillon, raced into the room. "Come quick and look what we found."

"Not now, little man," Jackson said, trying to use a soft tone. One of his biggest regrets since Julie had taken off was not being a better dad. He tried. Lord knew he tried, but lately, it seemed as if he and the boy spoke a different language. One Jackson was incapable of translating. "I had a rough shift. Where's your grandmother?"

"She had a lady meeting. She said to tell you supper's in the fridge. All you have to do is heat it up."

"Thanks, little man." With a deep sigh, Jackson collapsed onto the couch. "Now, turn down the TV and let me grab some shut-eye. We'll nuke dinner, then play catch when I get up."

"But, Dad, the TV's not on."

"Then turn down whatever it is that's making that noise."

Jackson shut his eyes, putting a throw pillow over his head. It smelled like maple syrup. He had to stop letting Dillon eat breakfast in the living room.

"But, Dad, that's what I've been trying to tell you."

"Son, please. Give me an hour and then we'll eat. Play catch. Whatever you want."

"Okay…"

Chin tucked against his chest, Dillon tried hard not to cry on his way to the kitchen.

He'd give anything to get his mom back home, because if she came back, his dad would be back, too. It hurt knowing his dad didn't love him anymore. Sometimes, late at night, when he heard his dad watching TV, he wondered if his father thought it was Dillon's fault Mom now lived in Kansas City? Was that why Dad was always grumpy? Because he blamed Dillon for all the bad stuff that'd been happening in their lives?

"Well?" Oliver asked out on the back porch. "Is your dad coming?"

Dillon shook his head. Tears were real close to squeezing out, so he didn't want to talk.

"What's wrong?" Owen asked. "You crying?"

Dillon shook his head.

"Then what's the matter?" Oliver put his hands on his hips. "Where's your dad?"

"He's sleeping, okay?" Snatching up the baby's basket, Dillon walked to the screened porch's door, bumping it open with his butt. "Let's just take the baby to your mom."

PEDIATRICIAN Ella Garvey climbed out of her minivan, marched up onto the frumpy Queen Anne house's front porch, threw open the screen door and walked directly to the freezer without passing Go. It'd been a chocolate-chip-fudge-mocha-swirl kind of day. Meaning, instead of using a teaspoon, she'd gone straight to the serving-spoon drawer after opening the ice cream tub's lid.

The first bite went down silky smooth.

Closing her eyes, she savored the cool, sweet goodness, letting the calories and fat seep into her weary bones. She'd get a fresh start on her diet tomorrow. Tonight would be about taking care of herself in a far more important way than the mere physical upkeep of her body.

After the day she'd had, actually having to be civil to her ex-husband's new bride—the same bride who'd once been her trusted best friend and office manager—well, she deserved not only ice cream, but pizza and bologna and chips and dip and Skittles and—

"Mooo-om!" The front door creaked open, then slammed shut.

As if that wasn't enough noise, the twins must've already turned on the TV, because along with boyish stomping came infant wailing.

Damn.

"I'm in here, guys!" She took another fortifying bite, scolding herself for wishing her darlings back at summer camp. She loved her twins dearly, but good grief, they could be a handful.

"Mom, Mom!"

"Slow down," she said, not wanting their haste to make a mess, which would in turn interfere with her medicinal feasting. "And for heaven's sake, turn down the—"

"Yeah, but look!" Oliver presented her with a sight that threatened to bring her ice cream gurgling up. "Can we keep it?"

"Oliver William Garvey, where in the world did you find her?" Tossing her spoon in the sink, setting the ice cream on the counter, Ella fell into professional mode. She plucked the red-faced, screaming, two- or three-week-old infant from a wicker laundry basket, instinctively clutching her to her chest.

"Shh…" she crooned, while jiggling and rocking the baby. Though she had a few hundred questions for her little darlings, first things first. "Oliver, get my medical bag from my office. Owen, fill a pan with hot water and put it on the stove."

"But you told me to never touch the stove."

"Do it!" she shouted above the din. "Dillon, honey, run to Owen and Oliver's closet and get me the smallest T-shirt you can find."

"Like one of those dumb Barney ones Owen used to wear in first grade that he hides way in the back?"

"Perfect," she said.

"They're not dumb," Owen complained.

"Here you go, Mom." Breathing heavily, Oliver handed over her bag.

"Thanks, honey." Placing the baby back in the basket, Ella found formula and a disposable bottle. She opened a can of Enfamil, slipped a plastic liner in the bottle's body, then popped a rubber nipple into the lid. After filling the bag with formula, she screwed on the lid.

Seeing that the water was close to boiling, she turned off the gas flame, set the pan on a cool burner, then dropped the bottle in.

Dillon dashed back into the kitchen. "Here's the shirt."

"Great. Oliver, fish me a diaper and some wipes from my bag."

"'Kay, Mom."

The bottom of the baby's pink pj's was soaked. Ella laid her on a towel on the kitchen table and removed the diaper, wiped the infant clean, then pulled Owen's purple shirt over her little head. As she'd figured, it was huge, but at least dry.

Next, she held the still-squalling baby on her hip while she tested the formula's temp. Perfect.

Ella cradled the baby, holding the bottle to her pursed lips. Rather than latching on, she seemed confused. It took the tiny creature a few minutes to figure out what to do. Probably a sign that she was used to being breastfed. Putting her pinkie to the infant's lips, Ella found that she'd suckle that. Placing the nipple alongside her finger, she tried tricking the infant into thinking she was back with her mom. Luckily, the poor thing must've been hungry enough that the ruse worked. The wailing stopped—and was replaced by near-desperate suckling.

"Whew," Oliver said, wiping his brow. "I didn't think she'd ever shut up."

"She must've been starving." Ella stroked the girl's blond tufts of downy hair. "Now, how about you gentlemen tell me how you got this angel?"

JACKSON WOKE SLOWLY, disoriented as to where he was. Splitting his time between the firehouse and home, rarely getting a full night's rest, he was used to catnapping. But lately, his sleep seemed to come on faster and harder. Deep and dreamless.

He rolled off the sofa, struggling to his feet.

Though he wasn't the least bit hungry, for Dillon's sake, he needed to make good on nuking his mom's meal.

His mother had been a godsend throughout the divorce. When he was on shift at the firehouse, she kept Dillon with her. His mom also saw to it that they ate pretty much three squares a day. There were times Jackson felt ashamed by how dependant upon her he'd become.

"Yo, Dillon!"

When the boy didn't answer, Jackson assumed he was outside, playing with his friends.

Peering out the front window, he found the moon rising on twilight. A few fireflies hovered above the half-dead lawn, and across the street, Joe Parker's legs stuck out from under his '63 Chevy. There were not, however, three boys playing catch or Frisbee or capture the flag.

Frowning, Jackson checked the kitchen, Dillon's room, the den where they kept the computer, the backyard where the boys staged naval battles in the six-inch-deep plastic pool. His son occupied none of his usual haunts.

Jackson was just picking up the phone to see if Dillon had gone to his folks' place when the doorbell rang. He hightailed it that way to see the shadowy figure of a woman behind the screen.

Upon closer inspection, he recognized Ella Garvey.

"Hey," he said, having to lift the broken-hinged door to get it to swing properly. "Come on in. I don't suppose you've seen Dillon?"

"Funny…" She laughed, only the sound came out more panicked than happy. "I was hoping you'd seen Owen and Oliver."

"I DON'T KNOW about this," Owen said, trailing behind Oliver and Dillon. He carried his mom's medical bag and formula and blankets while Oliver carried the baby and diapers and Dillon hauled towels and chips and pop and cupcakes.

"Quit whining," Oliver said, ashamed of his little brother.

"You're not the boss of me," Owen said. "This is a bad idea."

"I am too the boss of you," Oliver said, "and if you don't quit complaining, I'm not going to let you play my new Xbox game."

"Dad's not even gonna buy you that game," Owen fired back. "He loves me more than you."

"Does not."

"Does, too."

"Does not!"

"Zip it!" Dillon hollered. "Do you two dummies wanna wake up the baby?"

"Yeah, Owen." Oliver shot his brother a dirty look.

Owen rolled his eyes. "How much farther?"

They'd been walking a *really* long time, and they'd had to cut cross-country so no grown-ups would see. The stitch in Oliver's side hurt *really* bad, and though he wouldn't tell his twin or Dillon, he was kind of scared. It was getting dark and he'd never been this far from home without being in the car with his mom and dad. Now that his dad didn't live with them anymore, he hardly ever saw him. It used to make him sad that his father loved a new family better than him, but most times now, he was just mad.

Oliver was gonna be a way better dad to this baby than his own father was to him. Which was why when Mom said they had to call the police, and then she'd gotten on the phone, Oliver had told Owen and Dillon they had to run away.

Everyone knew when the police got you, you went straight to jail. What was a baby going to do in the slammer? They'd probably only feed her roaches and stuff and no way was he going to let *his* baby eat roaches. She was too cute for that.

"Please," Owen whined, "let's stop."

"Not yet," Oliver said, holding the baby tighter. "We're almost there."

"THEY FOUND *WHAT?*" Jackson liked to think he'd heard it all, but Ella's story was a bit far-fetched.

She explained about the boys having stumbled across the abandoned infant in the park. About the note attached to her basket. Through it all, he held his breath, waiting for the joke's punch line. Only, when Ella ended, her gray eyes pooling upon telling him all three boys and the baby were missing, he wasn't laughing.

In his line of work, tears were the norm, yet something about the way Ella looked near crying, but somehow keeping it together, affected him more than if she'd sobbed.

His ex had never cried.

Even on the day their divorce had been finalized, she'd remained coolly professional, as if to her, their marriage had been nothing more than a losing day in court. Just once, he'd wanted Julie to acknowledge what she'd thrown away. To have maybe at least come to him, cluing him in on the fact that there'd even been a problem. It'd hurt so damned bad knowing he couldn't save their marriage when *saving* was what he did. He rescued little kids and kittens and bedridden elderly. He didn't stand by, letting their lives end, any more than he gave up on vows he'd made before God and family. Julie was the only quitter in his house.

Frustrated anew by the uncomfortable position he found himself in, Jackson's voice was more gruff than it should've been when he asked, "Have you talked with Hank?"

Hank was a longtime friend and the town's sheriff.

"No," Ella said, looking away, then back. Wiping her eyes so he wouldn't see how upset she truly was? "Hoping the boys were here, I wanted to check with you first."

"Sure," he said, already on his way to the kitchen phone.

Five minutes later, Jackson had shared all pertinent information, and Hank had set official wheels in motion.

"Three boys and a baby," he said to Ella, who was again looking near tears. "They can't have gone far. We'll find them in under thirty minutes."

"I know." Her words were confident. Her thin voice scared.

What was it with women? Why couldn't they just say what they felt? Why couldn't she admit she was upset and ask for his help?

Maybe the better question was, what was it about her heart-breakingly concerned expression that made him care?

Chapter Two

Please, God, let Hank find them all safe. •

Ella had said the prayer hundreds of times during the endless night, but now, with the early-morning sun filling the boys' second-story bedroom, why did her throat ache worse than ever? Why, when Hank had told her to stay put, had she desperately wanted to help with the search?

The living room and kitchen teemed with concerned friends and family. Tables were laden with cold cuts, cookies and cake, as if food could somehow fill the gnawing emptiness that had consumed her since Jackson's promised thirty minutes had faded into ten hours without her boys.

As a doctor, she'd trained for all sorts of emergencies. Broken arms and legs she could handle, but this not knowing just might be the end of her.

A knock sounded on the boys' open door. "Your friend Claire said I'd find you up here."

"Jackson."

Hugging Owen's favorite stuffed tiger, she glanced the man's way. "Any sign of them?"

"A dirty diaper and a few granola-bar wrappers out by the old Hampstead place. Looks as if they may have camped there for the night, but no sign of them now."

She nodded, willing down the bile rising in her throat. "What's next?"

"A couple of hours ago, we called in help from Buckhorn County. About fifty National Guardsmen have also joined the search. My…um…ex has connections. She called in favors. It won't be long till we bring them home."

"I know," Ella said, adding a new wish to her litany of prayers—that she wouldn't break down now. Not in front of this virtual stranger.

"We've got tracking dogs. They're good."

I miss my boys. Please, God, bring them home safe.

Don't cry, don't cry, don't cry…

"I'm thinking thirty more minutes is all it's going to take. Tops."

"Y-you said that last time." Her eyes stung.

"Obviously, I underestimated, but this time—"

"This time, what?" she all but shrieked. "Do you have a crystal ball? Have you also called in a psych—" A sob racked her body. Tears flowed and she looked away, but then Jackson pulled her against him, wrapping her in his strength. As if she'd known him a lifetime, because exhaustion and terror and a sense of unbearable helplessness had taken a toll, she clung to him. "I—I'm so afraid," she cried. "W-what if you don't find them? Or, w-worse—"

"Shh…" He held her tightly, cupping his hand to the back of her head, as if sheltering her from the harsh realities of what had become of their world. "We'll bring them all back safe. If not in thirty minutes, then soon. Everything's going to be okay."

Because of the sureness of his tone, his powerful hold made her believe him. The worry gripping her insides refused to let her believe anything else.

Once her cheeks had dried and her labored breathing had

returned to normal, Jackson released her with an awkward pat to her back, stepping away.

"I should rejoin the others," he said, already edging toward the door.

She followed. "I want to go. I can't stand just sitting here. I feel helpless."

"Look…" He released a deep sigh. "On the off chance you're needed, you should stay."

"What do you mean?" she asked, gaze narrowed. "*Needed?* Why do I get the feeling you're trying in a polite way to prepare me for one or more of our boys needing medical attention?"

"All I'm saying is just in case. There's no sense in you being exhausted. Should the need for first aid—for anyone, be it the boys or the baby or one of the search party—arise."

Despite knowing Jackson was right in his request for her to stay put, Ella wasn't sure her heart could withstand one more moment of inactivity. "Please, Jackson, there must be something productive I can do."

"I suppose making sandwiches is out?"

Shooting him a sarcastic smile, she said, "There are already enough sandwiches downstairs to feed every man, woman and child in the state."

"Come on," he said, gesturing for her to follow. "I'll see what I can do."

"IT STINKS IN HERE," Owen said, looking up at the storm-drain tunnel's cobwebbed ceiling, then clutching his backpack tighter. "I'm hungry. Let's go home."

"We can't just go home," Oliver pointed out. Truthfully, deep inside his belly where the hunger pangs were starting to hurt really bad, he kind of wanted to go home, too. Eat a big plate of his mom's blueberry pancakes with one of those whipped cream smiley faces she drew on them. After that, he'd play video games, then crawl into his mom's big bed. She had more pillows than him and Owen. She'd asked if he wanted more pillows, but he'd said no, seeing how having his bed covered in soft stuff wouldn't be very manly. Since his dad had taken off and Oliver was oldest, that made him man of the house and in charge. He had to set a good example for his little brother, for Dillon and the baby. "If we go home, we're gonna get grounded and Daffodil's gonna get sent to jail."

"I still think that's a stupid name for a baby," Owen said, "and they won't take her to jail, but juvie."

"You're both wrong." Dillon hugged the sleeping infant. "She'll go to the *big house.* I saw it on TV. It's way worse than *just* jail or juvie. She'll probably have to be in a gang and stuff."

Oliver rolled his eyes. "She's a baby. How's she gonna be in a gang?"

"Gangs are smart." Dillon kissed the top of the baby's head. "My teacher, Mrs. Henseford, says gang leaders like to get their new members young."

"Please," Owen whined, "let's go home."

"No." Oliver pitched a rock at a tin can. "We have to get jobs—and a car."

"Yeah," Dillon said with a heavy sigh. "But before that, you guys ever come up with what we want to name her?"

"I already told you, Rapunzel," Owen said.

"That'd be fine," Dillon said, "only she doesn't have any hair."

"How 'bout Baldy?"

Dillon wrinkled his nose. "That's not very pretty. We have to give her a girly name."

"Fluffy? Kimmy? Cassie?"

"Nah," Dillon said. "I'm not feeling any of those."

"Okay, well if you don't like Daffodil, what about calling her Rose? Roses are pretty, and they smell nice."

"Yeah," Dillon said, "but most times, this baby smells bad."

"That's just because she poops a lot," Owen pointed out. "But she'll stop that when she's old."

"So you want to call her Rose?" Oliver asked.

Dillon gazed down at the baby girl and smiled. "Yeah. Rose…I think that sounds really pretty."

"THANK YOU," Ella said. The sincerity in her tone and warmth behind her eyes told Jackson he'd done the right thing in getting her a job manning the phone lines. "This has been good for me." She sighed. "You know—getting my mind off things for a while."

"Sure." Given the gravity of their shared *things*, he wasn't sure what else to say.

The police station's dingy beige lobby hummed with activity.

Phones ringing.

Teletype grunting.

Hank barking orders.

Not since grizzled old Digger Mason had been found dead under the Forked River bridge had Jackson seen such a commotion. Deputies had been called in from three additional counties. Bullock County had just suffered major tornado damage from a sudden spring storm and couldn't spare the manpower. With all available National Guard members also helping, using the station parking lot as a home base, Jackson had had to park half a block down the street.

A lot of the guys from the fire station had also come down to help with the search. Hank had mentioned that Jackson's best bud, Vince Calivaris, currently led a crew at the abandoned rock quarry. While Jackson thought it was good of

Calivaris to lend a hand, the thought of him finding the boys floating facedown in icy, deep-blue water filled his stomach with cold lead.

"Coffee, Mrs. Garvey?" Deputy Heidi Wesson offered Ella a steaming cup. "Fresh-brewed. Can I get you some cream or sugar?"

"No. But, thank you," Ella said, accepting the cup, cautiously sipping, then groaning with apparent pleasure. Jackson had never seen a woman take her coffee black. He supposed, what with her being a pediatrician and all, that she'd probably never had time for frivolities like doctoring a cup of joe. He found himself liking that fact about her. Her no-nonsense attitude.

You despise that quality in your all-business ex.

Did he? Or was it the fact that she'd valued efficiency over love?

"How about you?" Heidi asked, offering Jackson a cup, as well.

He murmured his thanks.

"If you're hungry, the PTA set up an amazing snack table in the break room. I heard it's being manned by parents from the boys' school, and that—"

"I—I have to go," Ella said, her voice faint. "Th-thanks again for the—" She gestured to the cup she'd set on a battered metal folding chair.

"Sure. No problem…" Heidi murmured while Ella ran for the building's double front doors. She pushed them open as if desperate for air. *Hope.*

"Want me to check on her?" Heidi asked Jackson. They'd been friends for a while. She'd started with the sheriff's office the same year he'd taken a full-time position with Firehouse Number 3. The town actually only had two fully manned stations. Number 1 was an honorary title given to the historic red barn holding dive gear for rare underwater rescues.

Shoulders squared, chest aching at the sight of Ella out on the station's concrete surround, hunched over, bracing her hands on her knees, Jackson said, "Thanks, but let me."

"Sure? I'm thinking this situation calls for a bit more finesse than your usual growling self."

"Give me a break," he said, setting his already emptied cup alongside Ella's.

"I'm just saying…" His friend held up her hands, flashing a wry smile.

He shook his head.

Outside, the day was fine. Bright and sunny. Not a cloud in the sky. Not at all the kind of day that suited his mood.

He aimed for Ella, but some GI Joe decked out in full-on camo gear beat him to the punch. He'd slipped his arm around Ella's quaking shoulders, giving her sympathetic pats.

Why, Jackson couldn't have said, but even from where he stood a good twenty feet away, possessiveness tore through him. He and Ella were going through this godawful ordeal together. He'd be the one to comfort her. See her through it. Guarantee all three of their boys and this baby they'd carted off were safely returned.

Marching to Ella's side, he cleared his throat and said to the guy still rubbing her back, "I'll take it from here."

"I'm good," the National Guardsman said.

Lowering his voice to the universal *back-off* tone, Jackson said, "Seriously. She's with me."

"Oh." The guy eyed Ella, then him, then backed away. "I was just trying to help."

"I know. Thanks."

"No problem."

Once the Guardsman had left, Jackson shoved his hands in his jeans pockets. He wanted to comfort Ella—damn bad—but something inside him felt broken. As if Julie had taken a chunk of him with her when she'd taken off.

"Look at me," Ella said with a messy sniffle. "I'm a bona fide wreck."

"I'd say you have a right to be."

"You're not. A mess, that is."

Wanna bet?

"Here we've both been trained to deal with all manner of emergencies, yet I'm falling apart."

"Correct me if I'm wrong," he said, "but they probably didn't teach you much in med school about what to do in the event your twins go missing."

She laughed through more tears, wiping her eyes with the backs of her hands. "You've got that right."

"Come on," he said, reaching for her hand. His movements were awkward, landing his knuckles against her thigh before fumbling for the tear-dampened fingers of her left hand. But once he had hold of her, he held on for all he was worth. "I'm meeting up with my ex in a little while, but for the moment, it looks like we're just in the way here. There's somewhere I think you should go."

"Just me?" Trailing beside him, her red-rimmed eyes were trusting, yet at the same time, wary.

"Well…" He squeezed her hand. "Obviously, we're both going. I've got my cell should there be any news."

"Good news," she said.

"Absolutely."

"Because that's the only kind we'll accept, right?"

Lord, how Jackson missed the days back when he used to be filled with hope. When he used to believe prayer really worked.

Back before Julie had left for greener pastures. He'd already lost his marriage. If he ended up losing his son, as well…

"Right, Jackson? Good news is all we'll take?"

He swallowed past the lump in his throat. "Uh-huh."

"How DID YOU EVER find this?" Ella whispered, oddly afraid to speak in her full voice, almost as if the wondrous place's spell might be broken.

"Accident," Jackson said with a shrug. "Long story short, we were working a three-car pile-up alongside the highway, and I needed to take a leak."

The answer was so unexpectedly honest—not to mention inappropriate—that she burst out laughing.

"What?"

"*You*. You're not exactly brimming with social graces, are you?"

"That a problem?"

"Considering what we're going through, not at all. However, once our boys are safely home, and we're back to our old routines, if you ever get a hankering to ask out Deputy Heidi, you may wish to bone up on your suave skills."

At that, he was the one laughing. "Thanks. It's been years since I've had that good a laugh."

"Let me guess. You've never exactly been brimming with suaveness, either?"

"Ding, ding, ding. You win the prize." He lifted a pine bough for her to step under.

No, judging by the present view, they'd both won.

They'd walked maybe a mile to where the small town faded to forest. To where historic brick homes eventually led the way to thousands of acres of farmland and sky. But here, in a secret glade time had forgotten, Ella stood gaping at the ghostly form of a paddle wheeler. Though the decades hadn't been kind, the iron behemoth was still elegant in its sea of stately oaks and pine. Listing slightly to the right, as if weary, like her.

"Jackson… It's amazing. Why…? How?"

"You mean what's it doing here?" he asked, flashing her a sad half grin. "A buddy of mine who's a history buff said back before the river was diverted, it used to run through this little valley. There's been talk of somehow salvaging her—turning her into a museum, but the amount of cash involved would be…" He whistled.

"Still—to think this has been here all this time. There should at least be a proper path leading to it."

He shrugged. "Probably that'd only encourage teens coming out here to drink and do miscellaneous other dirty deeds."

"Yeah… You're probably right."

For a few moments they quieted, absorbing the forest's tranquility. A woodpecker hammered a nearby tree, breaking the stillness.

"Why'd you bring me here?" Ella asked.

He crammed his hands in his pockets, looking away. "When my wife—well, when she asked for a divorce…"

"This place brought you solace? You thought it might do the same for me?"

He glanced down, then up. His dark eyes were wet.

He didn't deny her assumption.

Many times, when Julie and Jackson had struggled to save their marriage, Dillon had stayed with Ella, Todd and the twins. Ella's had been the shoulder Dillon had cried upon, meaning she knew far more about the end of Jackson's marriage than he would probably feel comfortable with.

"Thanks," he said quietly, taking a seat on a moss-covered fallen tree.

"For what?" She approached the boat, staring up in wonder.

"Being there. For Dillon." He cleared his throat. "That kind of hostile environment. I'm sure you know it's no place for a kid. He was just a little guy back then."

"He still is," she said, stepping up beside the shell of a man Jackson had become. She had few memories of him from before his divorce. A couple of neighborhood picnics with Dillon riding on his shoulders and Julie trailing behind, chatting on her cell. Upon ending her call, she'd run laughing to catch up, taking Jackson's hand, grinning up at him with what Ella had always assumed was love. They'd had their differences, but from the outside it had seemed like a sweet family.

Not that Jackson and Dillon weren't still a family, but not nearly as idyllic. As happy.

When Jackson remained silent, she gave him a slight nudge. "He's still just a little boy, Jackson."

"You think I don't know that?" His voice was hoarse.

"Hey," she said, placing a hand lightly on his shoulder, "I didn't mean that as a critique of your parenting skills. It was just an observation. At times—when Dillon thinks no one's looking—he seems…I don't know—crushingly lonely."

"Yeah, well, aren't we all?" Pushing to his feet, Jackson said, "I'm heading back. Stay as long as you like, and if I hear anything, I'll—"

"I'm coming with you." She was on her feet, as well.

"You don't have to."

"Of course, I do. For better or worse, we're in this together and—"

"Don't…ever…say…that." Though he didn't turn to face her, he squared his shoulders as if readying for a fight.

"Say what? *We're in this together?*"

He took off walking. His long-legged stride was tough to keep up with, but not impossible.

"Damn you," she said, snagging the sleeve of his navy polo. "What's the matter with you? You act like a walking shell. You can't just throw something like that out there without—"

Jackson's cell rang.

Chapter Three

"What've you got?" Jackson asked, pulse raging upon seeing Hank's number on his cell's Caller ID.

"Great news. We've found 'em. All four tired and dirty, but safe and sound."

Relief made Jackson fall to his knees.

"Jackson?" Ella demanded, kneeling beside him. "What is it? Are they hurt?"

Tears he never indulged in flowed.

He pulled her into a hug, burying his face in her hair. "They're safe. Dillon, your boys—even this mystery baby. All safe."

He'd started to release her, but now she was crying, quivering, so he held on for dear life. Celebrating life. The lives of their sons. His own life which had miraculously been returned.

"I can't believe it," she said, pulling away slightly, her happy, teary smile making her face glow. "I mean, I can. I knew they'd be safe—wanted to hope. But the fear, it took over."

He nodded. "I know. Wanna go get them? Hank took them to the station. No doubt loading them with candy bars and cookies."

"Hmm…" she teased, already rising, laughter crinkling the corners of her eyes as she held out her hand to help him.

"With all those sweets in them, maybe we should leave them there till they come down from the sugar high?"

OLIVER DIDN'T WANT TO CRY when he first saw his mom running with Dillon's dad toward him and Dillon and Owen, but as hard as he tried being big, being in charge of two kids and a baby for all that time had taken a lot out of him.

"Mommy!" Owen said, changing to his baby voice, like when he was scared of storms. He got to her first, throwing his arms around her waist. "I missed you so bad. I was starving and Oliver was mean and—"

"I wasn't mean. I even gave you the last bite of that granola bar and—"

"Did not!" Owen complained. "And anyway, get back. I'm mad at you."

"You get back! And quit hogging Mom." Oliver nudged his creepy twin out of the way, grabbing hold of her himself. Squeezing really hard, he closed his eyes and sighed. Man, she smelled nice. Like those good-smelling dryer-sheet thingies she used.

"I missed you so much," she said, hugging them both.

"Yeah, but you missed me more, right?" Owen pushed in closer. Geez, he was a spoiled brat.

"I'm oldest, so she missed me more, since she's had me around longest."

"Hey," Mom said, scrunching down so she was the same height as them. "I missed both of you more than I can ever say." She was crying and wiped at her eyes. Oliver hated seeing her cry. He especially hated that him and Owen had been the cause. But they'd had to protect the baby. "That said, I've never been more furious with you both. What were you thinking? Running off like that?"

Ella stood, hands on her hips. "You should be ashamed. How many times have I told you that if you have a problem, always to come to me?"

"It was *his* idea!" both boys said at once, pointing to each other.

"You are *sooo* lying!" Owen said. "Just trying to get me in trouble."

"You're trying to get me in trouble," Oliver said.

"I don't care which of you came up with the bright idea to run off," Ella said. "I'm equally furious with you both." Still, she couldn't resist pulling them into another group hug, planting kisses atop their grungy heads. She loved them so much. An impossible-to-calculate *much* only a mother could understand.

But then she looked across the crowded police station to Jackson standing with Dillon in his arms. Looks like dads understood love, too. The boy rested his head on his father's strong shoulder and was sucking his thumb. Dillon hadn't done that in at least a year. The fact that he'd reverted to the old habit spoke volumes for how scared he must've been out on the run.

Though the station was a flurry of activity of National Guardsmen packing up equipment, and police slapping each other on their backs for a job well done, Jackson and his son had formed an island of serenity in a frenzied storm.

In all the years Ella had known the man, never had she seen him look more at peace. Well, obviously aside from when he and Julie had still been a couple. But that was a long time ago. He'd been a different man. Just as back then, still with Todd, she'd been a different woman.

"Mommy?" Owen tugged on her shirt. "Can we go home?"

"What about the baby?" Oliver asked. "We can't just leave her here."

"She's at the hospital with Dr. Shepherd," Ella explained.

"But I thought you're a baby doctor."

"I am, sweetie, but Sheriff Hank figured I'd probably want to spend time with my own babies tonight."

"I'm not a baby," Oliver pointed out.

"I am," Owen said. "I'm never running— Hey, look! There's Dillon's mom. And she's crying and hugging his dad. They getting married again?"

The polite thing to do would be to grant them privacy, so how come Ella felt riveted to the sight of Jackson and his ex?

"WANT ICE CREAM for dinner?" Jackson asked his son. The light at the intersection of King and Pine turned yellow. Easing to a stop, he added, "Banana split. Hot-fudge sundae. You name it."

Dillon shook his head.

"What's up, bud?" The light turned green, and Jackson accelerated. "You sick?" He reached across the SUV's front seat to feel his son's forehead. "You don't have a fever. Stomach ache?"

"Nah. I just miss Mom. And the baby. Think she's okay?"

"Mom? Or the baby?"

"The baby. I know Mom's okay, 'cause she said she'd be home when we get there."

Swell.

"The baby's fine. Hank said they're going to keep her at the hospital nursery until someone claims her."

"What's that mean?"

"Comes to pick her up. Hank's hoping maybe her mom or dad will have second thoughts about leaving her."

"I don't know…"

"What?"

"Well, if her parents left her in a basket on the merry-go-round, do they deserve to get her back?"

Jackson sighed. "Good question." Guilt rumbled through him at his own less-than-stellar parenting skills since Julie left.

"Dad?"

"Yeah?" Jackson pulled the car into their driveway, glad to be home. Gladder still for his son to be safely home, for this second chance to prove how much he loved him.

"Do you think maybe we could keep her?"

"The baby?" He killed the engine.

"I'd take care of her. You'd hardly even know she was here."

Laughing, ruffling his boy's dirty hair, Jackson said, "If she's half as noisy as you were when you were a baby, trust me, the whole neighborhood would know she's here."

Dillon made a face.

Jackson made one right back.

He'd only been teasing with his son, but the scowl settling around his lips as Julie pulled her silver Mercedes convertible into the single-lane drive was the real deal.

"I DON'T KNOW, HANK..." On the phone, Ella looked to her boys—finally clean and not bickering, seated at the kitchen table eating salad swimming in ranch dressing. While they'd been playing with their action figures in the tub, she'd cleaned away the remnants of having a house full of concerned neighbors. Claire, from a few houses down, had offered to help with the dishes, but Ella had politely refused. Call her crazy, but it felt good doing something homey and domestic. "I've just gotten this place feeling back to normal. What am I going to do with a—"

The doorbell rang.

"Just a minute," she said, "someone's ringing the bell."

Covering the mouthpiece of her cordless phone, she jogged

to the living room. Pushing at the front screen door—in muggy weather it tended to stick—she frowned at her first glimpse of the man standing on her porch.

She pressed the phone's off button.

"Don't tell me," she said, taking the pink-swaddled baby from Hank's outstretched arms. "The hospital's nursery was full?"

"Damnedest thing," Hank said, hefting two huge sacks of baby gear inside. "Three gals gave birth this afternoon. The place is swamped. Anyway, I really could use your help, Ella. Odds are, whoever this cutie belongs to, she's not far away, and we're quietly checking into things."

"What does that have to do with me?" Ella asked, gingerly taking a seat on the couch.

"I don't want this beauty ending up in the system, you know."

Ella rolled her eyes. "Oh, come on, Hank. Look at her. She's gorgeous. Do you have any idea how many couples are out there, begging to adopt newborns? Claire and Jeremy Donaldson have been trying for years to conceive. She's a second-grade teacher at the twins' school and her husband's an amazing carpenter. Lately, they've been looking into adoption. Maybe you should take her to them?"

"Sounds like a good call, but I'm not exactly playing by the book. If I get Child Protective Services involved, everything's going to get messy. It'd just be overall easier if you'd keep her for a few days until the birth mother is back in her right mind and comes to claim her."

"Hank…" Ella warned. "This mother left her newborn infant in a basket on a playground. Does this really sound like the move of a responsible parent?"

"You've got a point. But look how clean the kid was when your boys found her. The polite note. That tells me there's love involved. What if this girl's young? Scared? Didn't anyone ever give you a second chance?"

"Anyone ever call you a big softy?"

"DILLON, GUESS WHAT," Oliver whispered into the phone, checking around the corner to make sure his mom wasn't spying.

"What?"

"We're keepin' Rose."

"No way! That's not fair. How'd you get her?"

"Sheriff Hank just brought her over. Wanna come play? You can eat here. We've got tons of food."

Dillon was quiet for a little while.

"Well?" Oliver asked. "Are you coming?"

"I don't know. Mom's here and Dad's been acting weird. Wanting to play games with me and stuff. I think he wants me to hang with him. But then Mom's wanting me with her, too. I should probably stay here."

"Bring both of 'em. That way, they can play with Mom while we're playing with Rose."

"Sure it's okay with your mom?"

"Yeah. She likes having company. Plus, she's always wanting us to eat, so now she can feed you guys, too. It'll be fun."

BEHIND THE WHEEL of his SUV, Jackson killed the engine, then shot a glance in the rearview mirror at his son—engrossed in a handheld video game.

Jackson sighed, then rubbed his face with his hands.

"You all right?" Julie asked from beside him, a beribboned wine bottle on her lap.

"Sure. Long day—and night."

"No kidding. Sorry it took me so long to get here. Judge Parker wouldn't recess, so—"

"It's fine. You're here now, which is all that matters."

She flashed him a smile and patted his thigh.

To say Jackson had been surprised by Ella's impromptu dinner invite would've been the understatement of the week. His reaction had actually been more in the realm of shock. He felt badly about the way things had gone down in the woods—his getting all bent out of shape at her benign comment.

But shoot, for the most part, he felt as if even on a good day, he wasn't exactly playing with a full emotional deck. On a day like today? When he hadn't known if his son was alive or dead? Then Julie shows up, suddenly playing the part of concerned mom.

Let's just say Ella had been lucky his outburst hadn't been worse. Or maybe he was the lucky one, so that he didn't look like even more of an insensitive jerk.

"Come on, Mom and Dad." Dillon leaned into the front seat. "Let's go. I'm hungry."

"Sure," Jackson said with a start, wishing the longer days of late spring didn't also mean glaring sun at an hour when he'd have preferred the more soothing black of night.

While Jackson helped Julie from the tall vehicle, Dillon hopped from the car and raced across the yard. On the front porch that was decked out in red geraniums and white impatiens, Dillon didn't bother ringing the doorbell, but instead, tossed open the screen door and walked right in. "Owen? Oliver? Where's the baby?"

"Dillon?" called a female voice from inside.

Having ushered Julie onto the porch, then following, Jackson felt somewhat voyeuristic watching through the screen as Ella approached his son only to pull him into a hug. She'd changed from the jeans and T-shirt he'd last seen her in to white

shorts and a pink tank. She'd washed her long hair and pulled it into a ponytail, the ends of which were still damp.

"What're you doing here, sweetie?" she asked. "I would've thought you and your mom and dad would be having a special family night?"

"Nah. Owen and Oliver invited us for dinner. They said you'd be cool with it. 'Kay?"

"Um…sure, but—" She glanced outside, and Jackson lurched back. To what? Hide? "Jackson? That you?"

"Yup." He resisted the urge to smack his forehead for not having called to confirm that the dinner invitation had been from Ella and not the twins. "And Julie."

"Oh—hi. What a nice surprise. Come in." She tried opening the screen, but it didn't budge.

"You have to lift and then kick," Dillon pointed out, nudging her aside to complete the task himself. "It's almost, but not quite, broken, just like at our house."

"Thanks," she said, ruffling Dillon's hair. "Sometimes I forget."

"Ours is broken?" Julie asked.

"I'm on it," Jackson said, marveling at the woman's gall to call his home *ours*.

"Come on, Dad. Owen and Oliver said there's lots of good food."

"I'm sorry," Jackson said to Ella. "Dillon said you'd invited us, but clearly he must've misunderstood."

"Dillon!" Oliver said, cautiously maneuvering the front staircase, the baby in his arms. "Look how pretty she is in her little dress. The ladies at the hospital gave it to her."

Ella turned. "Be careful with her, Oliver."

"*Awww…*" Dillon raced in that direction. "She's so cute."

"She's amazing," Julie crooned. "Dillon, I don't remember you ever being this tiny."

"You might as well stay," Ella said. "The neighbors were crazy generous with food."

"They're good folk," Jackson said. "They did a lot for me after…"

My wife took off.

Ella, still holding open the door, cleared her throat and stepped aside. "Come on in. I'll get out the plate of cold cuts and some bread."

Jackson followed the two women to the kitchen. He didn't want to be here. Forced into making small talk with a neighbor he hardly knew and the ex he more often than not wished he'd never known.

"Mayo or mustard?" Ella asked in front of the fridge.

"Both," Jackson said.

"Nothing for me," Julie said.

"Hey, Dad!" Dillon hollered, rushing into the room, the baby in his arms. "Guess what?"

"You need to slow down." Jackson gestured to the pink bundle. "The, ah, well, baby's fragile."

"Duh, Dad. And her name is Rose. We named her after the flower."

"Here, Mom—" Grasping the infant under her arms, Dillon gingerly handed her to Julie.

Julie tucked the baby against her chest and began to coo. "Aren't you a sweetie pie? Yes, you are…"

"She likes you," Ella said to Julie. "That's a good sign that you make her feel loved and safe."

Loved and safe? Ha! It took everything Jackson had in him

not to snort. How about the emotional number she'd pulled on their son?

Still, watching Julie with Rose sent him back to when Dillon had been a baby. To when he and Julie had been overwhelmed with the enormity not just of the logistics of bathing, diapering and keeping up a steady supply of mushy carrots and peas, but love. The love they'd both felt holding their infant son in their arms, or lying in bed with him early mornings, wondering what went on behind his enormous brown eyes.

Jackson glanced up to find Ella staring his way. He cast her a faint smile. They shared a kinship of sorts, as they both belonged to the cheating spouse club. Granted, Julie's lover had been her job, but it'd destroyed their marriage all the same.

Ella smiled back, making him feel even more lousy for the way he'd acted that afternoon.

The three boys each snagged a sandwich from a plate of them Ella had already made, then dashed out the back door. A few years earlier, Ella's ex-husband, Todd, had installed a wooden swing, slide and clubhouse combo. The guy was a jackass for having cheated on Ella, but apparently, the neighborhood kids still got a kick out of his handiwork.

"She does like you." Ella leaned against the counter.

"Thanks," Julie said. "I'd forgotten how wonderful babies are. Like a fresh start in human form."

"I've never heard it put quite that way," Ella said, "but sure, you're right."

The back screen door creaked open, and in ran Oliver. Face flushed, he asked, "Is it all right if we take Rose to show her to Whitney? She doesn't believe we have a baby."

"I suppose it's fine. But I don't want you leaving our street."

"May I have her?" Oliver asked Julie.

"Um, sure." Before handing her over, she kissed the top of

Rose's head. It was a fleeting thing. Barely even noticeable if Jackson hadn't been staring right at her. But curious all the same. Parental instinct kicking in?

"Thanks. Bye!" Oliver was off.

"Slow down!" Ella called after her son.

"Whew," Julie said, fanning her face. "Being responsible for that tiny life for even a few minutes was exhausting. Remember, Jackson, how tough it was with Dillon when he was a baby?"

"Sure."

"And, Ella, I can't imagine how difficult it must've been for you—with twins."

Ella chuckled. "*Difficult* is an understatement. There were times Todd and I wished we could send them back. But now," her expression turned wistful, "I wouldn't trade them for the world."

"I feel the same," Jackson said. "About Dillon."

Had Ella imagined it, or had the man's statement been loaded with animosity? Ella had many times wondered how Todd could've left their boys, happily trotting off to start a new family. She could never even conceive of such a thing. Yet in a sense, Julie had done the same.

"Where, ah, is your restroom?" Julie asked.

Ella directed her to the powder room tucked beneath the front stairs.

Though she'd been exasperated with Jackson that afternoon, Ella now softened. Jackson might be a bear on the outside, but on the inside, she suspected he was a spooked puppy, growling at what most scared him. And at the moment, what scared him more than anything in the world was love. Kindness of any kind. With Julie, he'd been happy. Complete. Then, like Todd, Julie had shattered that happiness, yanking the rug out from beneath him. Whether he knew it or not, strictly from a professional point of view, she suspected the man was emotionally floundering.

Not that Ella was one to talk, seeing how since the divorce, her ice cream addiction had resulted in twenty extra pounds.

"Tell me something," she said after Julie had left.

"What?" Jackson sat at the kitchen table.

"Earlier today, in the woods, when you got all huffy with me. What about the phrase, *for better or worse*—aside from the obvious broken wedding vow connection—set you off?"

Jaw clenched, hands fisted, he said, "Unless you're deliberately trying to set me off again, kindly drop it."

Chapter Four

"No," Ella said, chin raised, hands on her hips. "I'm not going to just drop it. Jackson, you need to—"

"Don't tell me what I *need* to do, when—"

"Ah, that's better," Julie said in a breezy tone, sailing into the kitchen. "Seems like the older I get, the more time I spend in the loo." Snatching a carrot from a veggie plate, she eyed Jackson, then Ella. "Did I miss something?"

"No," Ella said, turning toward the sink, thankful to no longer be in the line of Jackson's challenging stare. What had gotten into her even to care what his problem was? Obviously, the guy had a chip on his shoulder the size of Montana in regard to his ex.

"I like what you've done with the kitchen," Julie said, suddenly alongside her, reaching for the dishtowel to lend Ella a hand. "I've always loved a yellow kitchen. It somehow makes everything feel better."

"Do you own a home in Kansas City?" Ella asked, more out of a wish to be polite than because she honestly cared. For what the woman had so selfishly put Dillon through, Ella didn't think she'd ever consider Julie Tate a friend.

"Not yet. But lately, I've been thinking about it. The condo

I rent is gorgeous, but bland. Very beige. I miss putting my own decorative touch on things."

"Sure," Ella said, reaching for one of the boys' dirtied salad bowls. One of these days, she really had to get around to buying a dishwasher.

"With our house here, Jackson and I used to do projects every weekend. Remember, hon? That time we tiled the master bath floor, we got all the way through before we noticed the pattern was crooked."

From his seat at the kitchen table, Jackson grunted.

Was Julie hurting him with her trip down memory lane?

"Anyway," Julie continued, "as big a pain as that was, in the end, the floor looked gorgeous. I miss that bathroom. The tall windows. My master bath in K.C. doesn't have even one window. Makes me crazy not being able to see outside."

"I don't blame you," Ella said, handing her guest a freshly rinsed salad bowl to dry.

Jackson asked, "Should I check on the boys?"

"Why don't I do it?" Julie set the dishtowel on the counter. "I'd like to spend as much time as possible with Dillon while I'm in town."

A few minutes after she'd left, Jackson cleared his throat. "That was fun."

"Sorry," Ella said, not sure what else to say. "For what it's worth, I feel your pain in suddenly finding yourself stuck with your ex. Todd and his blushing bride came in the clinic the other day with Ben."

"Is that their little boy?"

"Yep." Fighting past the lump in her throat, Ella returned to her dishes. Maybe it was a good thing she hadn't gone dishwasher shopping. Scrubbing gave her something to do other than dwell on personal problems. "He was due for his one-year checkup. Todd never once went to one of the boys' doctor appointments, yet that day, with Dawn, he was the very embodiment of fatherly perfection."

"Wow." Jackson rubbed his jaw. "And here I thought I had it rough hearing my ex recalling home-improvement hell like it was time spent skipping through daisies."

Ella couldn't help but laugh. "Daisies?"

"You know what I mean." Getting up from the table, he snatched the dishtowel and dried the plate she'd just rinsed. "The woman makes me crazy. She's the one who ended our marriage, yet it seems like every time she blows into town to see Dillon, she's filled with nothing but happy memories. She wears blinders when it comes to our last year. The hell she put all of us through."

"Not that it's any of my business—" Ella said, draining the suds from the sink, then rinsing "—and, please, feel free to tell me to butt out, but why couldn't she practice law here?"

He snorted. "Said it was boring. She wasn't being challenged."

"I suppose for her field of criminal law, defending the occasional jaywalker or underage drinker would get dull."

"But what about me and Dillon? Were we *dull?*"

"Jackson…" Ella hefted herself onto the counter, letting her legs swing. "Don't take this the wrong way, but did you ever think of moving to Kansas City to be with her? I mean, they do have firemen there, don't they?"

He exhaled sharply, then looked away.

"What's wrong? Another sore subject?"

Posture defeated, he shook his head. "Don't think I didn't suggest the same thing. But she turned me down. Fed me some nonsense about how if we were with her, she'd feel

honor bound to spend time with us instead of working her way up the proverbial ladder. Can you imagine?"

Ouch. Todd had at least left her and the boys for lust. But to be abandoned for work?

Ella pressed her lips tight, hopping off the counter to give Jackson a hug. "I'm so sorry. You deserve better."

"We both do," he murmured into her hair.

Ella had meant the hug to be comforting. Purely platonic. But something about the warmth of Jackson's breath on her neck made her insides quiver. Awareness flooded her. A hypersensitivity to his size. His all-male smell. The way his hold wrapped her like a blanket—which was madness. She already had more than enough quilts in the upstairs linen closet, thank you very much. After Todd had left, she'd promised herself never again to turn to a man for emotional support. Sure, she might one day be in another relationship, but never again all the way. Heart and soul. Todd's infidelity had come damn near close to destroying her, and for the boys' sake, she had to learn to depend on herself.

Releasing Jackson, she turned her back to him, straightened the flyaways in her hair while willing her pounding heart to still.

It had just been a hug.

So what if her stomach had somersaulted?

Obviously, judging by their earlier conversation, Jackson still had feelings for his ex-wife. Meaning? Simply that when Ella finally felt comfortable enough in her own skin to rejoin the dating scene, Jackson would be a lousy first candidate.

"Thanks," he said.

"For what?" Her mouth had become the Sahara.

"Listening. Being here. For always having been such a good friend to Dillon, and now me."

She shrugged, not trusting herself to meet his gaze. "No biggie."

"Yeah, well, it is to us." Landing a playful slug to her right shoulder, he added, "You're a good gal."

A good gal? Nice. *Way to make me feel like a desirable woman.* Not that that's what she expected him to think of her, just that he certainly had a knack for making her feel decidedly undesirable.

Hand clamped to her forehead, she said, "I'm, ah, really tired. How about we track down our respective kids and call it a night?"

"We good?"

"Sure. Why wouldn't we be?" She gave him a bright smile.

"Hey…" Hand warmly clamped to her shoulder he said, "Even I know that's not your real smile."

"How would you know that?"

"Because at the exact moment we found out the boys were safe, I was privy to the real deal." Flashing a heart-tugging grin all his own, he winked. "I like that one much better." After squeezing her shoulder, he tucked his hands in his jeans pockets, then whistled his way to the back door. "Once I find our crew, I'll send yours home."

"THAT WAS NICE," Julie said while Dillon, still hyped up on the thirty-eight cookies he'd apparently downed at Whitney's house, jumped in front of the stuck screen door.

"You should fix that, Dad," his kid said, still jumping and not even breaking a sweat.

"I'll get right on it," Jackson said, giving the stupid thing a hard enough yank to pop off the bottom hinge, too.

"Honey," Julie complained, while he hefted the screen door out of the way, leaning it against the side of the house. "Look what you did. If you'd just let me do it, it wouldn't have broken. All you had to do was lift and jiggle."

Jackson took a deep breath and counted to ten.

She brushed him aside, then slid her key into the main door's lock. It irked him to no end that she even had a key.

Dillon shot by. "I'm gonna go play with my Xbox, 'kay?"

"What you're going to do," Julie shouted after him as he dashed up the stairs, "is get in the tub, then head straight to bed. Tomorrow's a school day."

"Aw, man…"

"Do it," Julie said, presumably in the same scary, I-mean-business tone she used on her new hardened-felon friends.

Jackson tossed his keys on the entry-hall side table, releasing a sigh. "Jules… You can't just waltz in here—"

"You called me Jules," she said, nestling her designer purse alongside his keys before sliding her arms around his waist and resting her cheek on his chest. "It's been a long time since you've called me that."

"Don't read anything into it. It's been an endless day, and I'm tired."

"I know what would make you feel better…" Easing her hands under his shirt's hem, she palmed his abs. There had been a time when her lightest touch instantly had him hard. Now? It didn't faze him. "Mmm…I see you've been working out."

"Okay," he said, royally ticked she'd pull this kind of stunt. Lightly grasping her wrists, he pushed her away. "I've officially had all I can stomach of whatever twisted game you're playing. First, you waltz in here, acting like you're our kid's mom when—"

"I am, and always will be, his mother."

"You gave him up, remember?" *Along with me.*

"Stop. You're not being fair."

"Fair? Julie, you freakin' walked out on us both. It's been

three weeks since you've even called Dillon to say hi, yet now you actually care whether or not he has a bath? Give me a break."

"No, you give me a break. Just because I—"

"Mom? Dad?" Jackson had been so engrossed with telling off his ex, he hadn't noticed his son sneaking up alongside them. Make no mistake— Dillon was *his* son. "I thought you weren't going to fight anymore."

Running his hands through his hair, not having a clue what to say to his little boy, Jackson headed for the kitchen.

"That's real mature!" Julie shouted after him. "Just walk away when our son is crying out for help!"

Oh—now she wanted to play the maturity game? With everything in him, Jackson wanted to tell this woman—this destroyer of their lives—just what he truly thought of her. But then he caught sight of Dillon. The way his lower lip trembled. Heart aching, Jackson went to his kid, easily lifting him into his arms.

"I love you," he said quietly in Dillon's ear. "Everything's going to be all right. Promise."

Dillon squirmed and bucked against him. "Put me down. I want Mommy."

Jackson did put Dillon down, silently watching while Dillon ran to Julie for a hug. But whereas he'd have fully expected Julie's expression to be triumphant, the gaze she shot over their son's shoulder was remorseful and threatening tears.

Tears? Was such a thing even possible from the woman he'd secretly dubbed the Ice Queen?

"Hey, bud," Jackson said, clearing his throat when his voice came out hoarse. "You need to get on with that bath."

"I will, Dad, but first, you have to promise not to fight anymore with Mommy."

Jaw tight, Jackson nodded.

"And, Mommy," Dillon said, eyes wide and shining, "you have to come be with us more, okay?"

"I will, angel." She kissed the crown of his head.

Once again, Dillon was off. This time, accompanied by the groan of the upstairs bathroom pipes when the tub water was turned on.

"I'm sorry," Julie said, sitting on the staircase's third step.

"No apology necessary. Let's just leave the past in the past."

"No," she said with a firm shake of her head. "When you told me Dillon was missing… I swear to God, my life flashed before my eyes. I mean, I know this will sound clichéd, but in that instant, everything faded except what's important—real. Dillon. You."

Tilting his head back in what he assumed would be a futile attempt to work the kinks from his aching neck, Jackson ignored the last part of Julie's speech. How many times when the ink had still been wet on their divorce papers had he prayed to hear those very words? But that had been a long time ago. He wasn't the same man. She'd emotionally destroyed him, and it would take a lot more than pretty words to put him back together.

"Well?" She gazed up at him with the same big brown eyes as their son. In the entry hall's dim overhead light, she'd never looked more beautiful, or, at the same time, more treacherous. Like quicksand, exploration would be foolish. "Aren't you going to say anything? Haven't you missed me?" .

"Sure, but—"

"When I saw you tonight with Rose in your arms, it took me back to when Dillon was a baby. You were such a great dad, Jackson—always a way better parent than me. But when it came to my turn to hold Rose, it dawned on me that maybe this was a wake-up call. Maybe we should try again. Have another baby and remember the way things used to be before—"

"Before what, Jules? Before you took off? That's a lovely fairy tale you've spun, but what happens when you get bored? Only this time, you're abandoning two kids instead of one? How are you going to worm your way out of that?"

"Do you have to be cruel?" she asked, voice shaky while tears streamed down her cheeks. "I said I was sorry. No one's perfect."

Jackson wanted to be cruel.

More than anything, he wanted to hurt her as much as she'd hurt him.

But her tears were his undoing, and the rescuer in him took over. "Come here," he said, tugging her up and into his arms. "We're both tired. It's been a long day. Maybe this is all stuff that should be gone over tomorrow?"

Sniffling, she nodded against his chest. "I love you."

Not knowing if he loved her, hated her, or felt a mixture of both, Jackson kept quiet. In the morning, he'd have clarity. Right now, all he wanted was sleep.

AT ONE IN THE MORNING, Ella finally stopped even trying to sleep, tossed back the covers and aimed straight for the peanut butter and chocolate-chunk swirl she'd stashed in the very back of the freezer, hoping it would be safe from little hands.

Baby Rose had been up a good half-dozen times, leaving Ella feeling more like a zombie than a well-rested physician who had to be in the clinic by eight.

She'd just closed her eyes upon taking the first sinful bite of ice cream when a knock sounded at the back door. Startled, she jumped, nicking the roof of her mouth with the spoon.

Through the ruffled back-door curtains, she made out a man's figure. Heart pounding, she snatched the rolling pin from a jar filled with kitchen utensils, then flipped on the back porch light only to exhale in relief. Her late-night visitor was Jackson.

Unlocking the door, she asked, "What are you doing here? Is everything all right? Where's Dillon?"

"Everything's sort of fine," he said with a grimace, brushing past her, overwhelming her with his size. "As for Dillon, he's sound asleep. Julie's at the house with him."

"She slept over?" Ella couldn't keep from asking, her right eyebrow rising.

"No," Jackson said, face reddening. "It wasn't that kind of sleepover. She said because of all the National Guard guys in town, she couldn't get a motel room, so I set her up in the guest room."

"Oh." After setting the rolling pin on the counter, she plopped back down at the kitchen table, wishing she'd slept in a cute baby-doll nightie rather than a baby-stained T-shirt and thin cotton shorts. "Not to be rude, but why are you here?"

Eyeing the rolling pin, he grinned. "That could've hurt."

"I'm not accustomed to late-night—or, I guess that would be early-morning—visitors."

"Sorry. As much as I wanted to, I couldn't sleep, and if the wind's blowing the trees just right, there's a view of your kitchen window from my master bath. I saw you were up, and…" He shrugged. "Got another spoon?"

She got up to find him a utensil, then handed it to him where he sat in the chair alongside hers. There was something oddly intimate about the moment. The occasional kissing of their spoons, crickets singing through the open window above the sink. The way Jackson's hair was mussed and the sleepy look in his eyes.

"So," he said, piercing the night's quiet with the single syllable word. "Julie apologized. Burst into tears and said she wants to try getting back together."

"Th-that's wonderful," Ella said, more than a little taken

aback. "I mean, assuming that's what you want. I know that's what Dillon's been hoping for, but…" Her words trailed off as she searched Jackson's unreadable expression.

"You know, that's what's so weird about the whole thing. Being a family again feels like all I've ever wanted, but she hurt me. Bad. When I snapped at you out by the old paddle-wheeler—when you said 'for better or worse'—it was because for so long now, my marriage has been reduced to the *or worse* portion of our vows. With Dillon still having been gone, in that instant, I guess I felt as though if one more bad thing slammed me, I'd crack."

"But you didn't," she said, hand on his forearm. It was a friendly, comforting touch. So how come instead of feeling comforted back, there was gnawing sadness filling her? Maybe even jealousy that the one thing they'd had in common—lousy marriages—was to be no more. "For Dillon, you stayed strong. And now, it sounds as if all the pain Julie put you through may be over. Maybe you two can even work on that fresh start?"

Covering her fingers with his, he said, "Thanks. Your listening to my rambling means a lot."

Trying to make light of the suddenly heavy mood, she said, "Just wait till you get my bill. Hope you have good insurance."

He laughed, filling her spirit with the delicious, rumbling sound. How was it that Dillon and her twins had been long-time best buddies, yet she hardly knew Dillon's father? Stranger still, how, in the terrifying hours their sons had been gone, had their friendship blossomed to the point where Ella now felt as if she'd known Jackson forever?

"I should quit hogging your ice cream and let you get to bed."

"Yes, you should," she teased. But not because she resented sharing her late-night treat; because the more she was around him, the more she suspected he would be all too easy to fall for.

Chapter Five

"So then Mom said her and Dad are getting married again, and then we're gonna have a baby, too." In Owen and Oliver's fort, Dillon held Rose extra good, figuring he'd need the practice for when he was a big brother.

"Are you gonna get a boy or girl?" Owen asked, kind of quiet since his mom was out in the yard, too, watering flowers.

"I'm thinking I'm going to tell them I want a girl. Rose is awfully cute, and now that your mom figured out how to feed her and bath her and stuff, she doesn't seem to be so much work."

"Yeah, dummy," Oliver interjected, "that's 'cause somebody else is taking care of her for us."

Dillon stuck out his tongue. "Why do you always have to be so mean?"

"Maybe I like it," Oliver said, snatching up the toy cars he'd been playing with and heading for the sandbox behind the fort. Truthfully, he did feel a little mean about calling Dillon a dummy, but it was really unfair that Dillon's parents were getting back together, while his own dad had married someone else. Oliver guessed he liked Dawn okay, and Ben only looked a little like an alien, but it wasn't the same. Deep down, Oliver knew his dad was never coming home, and that hurt. Sometimes, late at night, when Owen was snoring, Oliver cried about it, but that was only in secret with the covers over his head.

"Mom says I can be in their next wedding." Dillon's voice carried through the fort's thin walls, making Oliver wish their fort was made of a cajillion rocks. "I'll wear a tuxedo and everything. It's gonna be cool. Owen, you can come if you want. But if Oliver's gonna be mean, he has to stay home."

"Will there be meatballs?" Owen asked.

"Heck, yeah," Dillon said, jiggling the baby. "At least, I hope so. It wouldn't be a very good party without your mom's meatballs."

"I don't even wanna go!" Oliver shouted up at his two ex-friends. "And I'm telling *Mom* not to make her meatballs for you!"

"GOT A SEC?"

Glancing up from a mountain of medical records still needing to be updated, Ella's mood brightened. "Jackson. What a fun surprise."

"Let's hope you still consider me fun after I grouse a little more about my ex." Half laughing, half groaning, he eased into one of two matching brown leather guest chairs facing her desk. He wore jeans and a navy fire department T-shirt that fit snugly from what she guessed were too many hot-water washes.

Not that she was complaining.

Overheated from what she hoped was sun streaming through her office window and not from Jackson's well-defined chest, she grabbed the nearest manila file to use as a fan.

"Oh?" she prompted, not especially wanting to discuss

Julie, but she swallowed her dislike for the woman in order to be a good friend.

"This morning, I figured she'd head back to K.C., having forgotten her sudden urge to become Super Mom, but man…" he shook his head "…was I ever wrong. I overslept, to find she'd not only gotten Dillon off to school, but cooked a big country breakfast."

"And those are bad things?" Ella asked, setting down the file, leaning forward in her chair. "Wish somebody would cook me a big breakfast, and Lord knows I could've used the sleep."

"You know what I mean," he said with a sigh.

"Yes, I get it. I imagine her sudden interest in family life is very confusing for your son." *Not to mention you.*

"That's a given. She said she wanted to stay a few days, but thankfully, her cell wouldn't stop ringing, and she took off."

"Think Dillon's going to be upset when she's not home after school?"

"I'm afraid so, which is basically why I'm here." He shot her a painfully attractive grin. "Don't suppose you have any professional parenting advice for me?"

"I don't know," she said with a teasing shrug. "What's in it for me?"

"Well…"

"I'm joking. I'd love to help you, in any way—"

"I grill a mean steak and baked potatoes," he interjected, shifting in his chair.

"Deal, but I was just about to say I'd help for free."

"Seriously, Ell," he said, toying with a mini-Slinky one of her favorite patients had given her for Christmas. "If you're too busy, I can always just call for an appointment, or—"

"Hey…" Reaching across her cluttered desk, she stilled his busy fingers, ignoring what was getting to be a disturbingly common flutter of attraction. "I love Dillon. Over the years, I've grown to think of him as my own. I'd be honored to help in any way I can. Moreover, I'm flattered you'd think to ask." She was also more determined than ever to squelch the absurd fascination for this man that kept cropping up every time he was around. He was her friend. Nothing more. Worse yet, because of her love for Dillon, she was honor bound to do all in her power to see Julie and Jackson reunited.

THIRTY MINUTES later, armed with sage advice for how best to handle his current situation with his son, Jackson knew he should be focusing on Ella's words, but at the moment, the only thing he felt truly capable of focusing on were the intriguing little creases at the corners of her mouth. She'd been gifted with full lips that smiled easily. He supposed he'd always found her attractive, you know, in a kids' mom kind of way. But lately, okay, most especially since he'd sat at her kitchen table with her at one in the morning, sharing ice cream, wondering at the messy glory of her hair, she had gone beyond attractive in his eyes to absolutely gorgeous.

"Jackson? Judging by your expression, you think I'm wrong?"

"Huh—oh, yes. One hundred percent." She frowned.

Bad answer?

Ella pressed on. "So then you think Dillon *shouldn't* spend more time with Julie?"

"I'm sorry. Could you please repeat the question?"

"Have you heard anything I've said?"

He swallowed hard when she did it again, pursing her lips into a crazy-cute pout he found himself wanting to kiss. Which was ludicrous. Ella was off-limits. At least until he figured out what—if anything—he felt for Julie.

"Jackson Tate. If I didn't know better, I'd say I was boring you." Rising from her desk chair, she playfully conked his head with a file.

Ha! If only that were the case. "I'm sorry," he said, faking a yawn. "I guess I'm just tired, seeing how a certain someone kept me up all night with her ice cream."

"Like I forced you into my kitchen in the wee hours of the morning?" She tried conking him again, but this time, he dodged. Out from behind her desk, she now stood alongside him.

It would've been all too easy to snag her about her waist, tugging her onto his lap for that kiss he'd been craving.

It would've been easy, but because of Ella's relationship with Dillon, because of Julie and the fact he was supposed to be thinking of reconciling with her, kissing the pretty doctor would've been wrong.

Which was why he cleared his throat, then said, "Seriously, thanks for your help. Over our steaks tomorrow night, I'm going to pick your brain again, only this time I'll take notes." On his feet, he pulled her into a quick, awkward hug of gratitude, then left as abruptly as he'd entered.

"Mom?" Owen asked. They were at Polk's Sporting Goods, shopping for the boys' spring baseball league. Rose was home, being watched by Claire Donaldson. Oliver was in the football aisle, dreaming of when he could play junior-high and high-school ball like his dad. Knowing Todd had broken two ribs and suffered a concussion during his days on the field, Ella couldn't say she wanted her boy playing, but she wouldn't stop him if that's what he truly wanted to do.

"Yes, hon?"

"Are you making meatballs for Dillon's dad's wedding? Because Oliver said you weren't."

"What?" She froze beside the aluminum bats. "Where did you hear that?"

"Dillon." He snatched a ball, tossing it from hand to hand. "We both love those fancy meatballs you make for parties and stuff. So can you?"

She'd just talked with Jackson like a few hours ago, so how was it that now all of the sudden his remarriage was at the point that Dillon was planning the menu? If that was the case, seeing how she now considered Jackson a friend, why wasn't she more happy for him? After all, he was still admittedly bitter about what Julie had done, but behind that bitterness, she suspected was a tremendous amount of love.

"*Mo-om?*" Owen whined.

"What, honey?"

"Are you making meatballs?"

"Um, sure, sweetie," she said. "If that's what Dillon wants."

"It is. Can I have this?" He held out a bat.

"Sure. Whatever you want." Worrying her lower lip, she imagined Dillon must be thrilled, but when had Jackson even had time to reach this decision?

"What about this?" He held out a batting helmet.

"Honey, whatever—just pick."

"Why're you grumpy?"

"I'm not," she said, kneeling to tie her left sneaker. "This is great. I know having his mom back will make Dillon really—"

"He's not still talking about the stupid meatballs, is he?" Oliver rounded the corner, loaded down with football pads and a helmet.

"What's with all the gear?" Ella asked.

"I'm playing football."

"When?" she asked, glad for the distraction from wedding planning.

Chapter Six

"I still don't get why you're so bent out of shape by this," Ella's nurse and best friend, Rachel, asked the next morning. "It's just dinner between friends."

"Yeah, a *friend* I could all too easily be attracted to." During a rare and wonderful lull between patients, they sat across a small table from each other in the clinic's kitchen/break room. On a long-ago weekend, Ella and Todd had painted the walls yellow just like her kitchen at home. What fun they'd had, flirting and laughing and dodging flicked paint.

"So? What's wrong with that?" The freckle-faced, platinum blonde blew a bubble with her nicotine gum. She'd tried stopping smoking many times in the past, but this time, she'd been cigarette-free for two months and Ella was hopeful it'd last. "Heaven knows you could use a good date."

"Why's that? My life's plenty hectic as is. Why on earth would I want to further complicate it with a man?"

"Yes," Rachel said, stirring four packets of sugar into her coffee, "but as you already pointed out, Jackson Tate's not just any man. Not only is he a hottie, but he rescues small children from giant hamster wheels."

"They weren't in a wheel, just—"

"I know, I know. I was making a joke. Something you seem incapable of."

Following a trick from her sons, Ella stuck out her tongue at her friend.

"That was real mature."

"Sorry. I'm having a hard time with this, and you're not helping."

Leaning forward, Rachel asked, "What do you want me to do?"

"Listen. Yes, this guy seems like perfection, but he not only has a lot of emotional baggage, but an ex-wife wanting to hook back up. Dillon's ecstatic. Even if Jackson found me attractive—which he doesn't—there's no way after the hell Todd's infidelity put me through, that I would turn around and actually become the *other* woman."

"That's ridiculous." After a sip of her coffee, Rachel added, "How do you even know Jackson wants to get back together with his ex?"

"Gee, maybe because he told me."

"Oh." Lips pursed, Rachel asked, "Any chance he was drunk?"

Ella tossed an empty sugar packet at her. "Big help you are. Next time I need help, remind me to call a psychic hotline."

"HEY, YOU GUYS, get away from the ditch!" Jackson flipped the baked potatoes on the grill. To Ella, he said, "Is it just me, or does it seem like our gentlemen have a knack for finding trouble?"

"They do." She was rocking Rose's carrier with her red-tipped toes. They were cute toes. A feature he couldn't remember ever having found irresistible in a woman before. "But then I guess if you asked my mom, I was always in trouble at their age."

"Me, too. But I bet you were adorable trouble—mud on

your cheeks, and Strawberry Shortcake bandages on both knees."

"Bite your tongue. I had superhero bandages, thank you very much."

"Ah, you were a tomboy?"

"Heck, yeah. None of that girly stuff for me." Rose stirred, emitting a few fitful cries. Ella scooped her from the carrier and into her arms, then dug a formula-filled bottle from her diaper bag.

"Need to warm it?"

"Nope. I already did at home." She held the bottle to the baby and Rose hungrily latched on.

The two looked heartbreakingly lovely in the fading light, citronella torches flickering, crickets chirping. The fieldstone patio had been a bear to tackle, but seeing his neighbors enjoying the fruits of his labor filled him with satisfaction.

"Did you ever get hold of Hank?" he asked, wondering how much longer they'd have the baby with them.

"I tried, but he's at a convention in Chicago. I asked your friend Heidi about it, and she said they've got a few leads as to who Rose's mother might be, but nothing she can share."

"Ah," he said with an exaggerated nod. "Top secret, huh?"

"Apparently."

They'd sat in companionable silence for a few minutes—save for the boys' occasional shrieks of "That was *sooo* out!"—when Jackson could no longer hold in the question that'd been burning him. "We ever going to talk about it?"

"What?" she asked, wiping milky dribble from Rose's chin.

"Why you did a sudden one-eighty about tonight."

She sighed.

"That was informational." After closing the grill's lid, he

stretched out on the padded lounge chair beside her. "Care to elaborate?"

"Not really. I'm busy. End of story."

He snorted.

"You don't believe me?" she asked, eyebrows raised.

"Should I?"

Glancing out to where the boys played stick ball at the far end of the big backyard, her expression was hard to read. Almost as though she wanted to tell him something but wasn't sure where to start.

"Ell, come on. After all we've been through together, you can tell me anything."

She laughed, not her usual bubbly laugh, but more in the range of a strangled chicken. "Oh no. This, I'm for sure taking to the grave."

"Now, I don't *want* to know, but *have* to." Leaning closer, planting an impromptu kiss to Rose's forehead, he said, "Come on. Spill."

"No," she said, cheeks charmingly flushed. "It's too embarrassing."

"Want me to tell you a horrible secret first?"

"Okay…" Rose had apparently had her fill, and let the bottle's nipple fall from her mouth. The way the infant then snuggled against Ell's breasts caused his mind to wander to topics best left alone. Things like whether or not Ella had breastfed the twins. She had beautiful breasts—high and perfectly shaped to fit in the palms of a man's hands. Mouth dry, he caught himself staring and looked away before his own cheeks reddened. "I'm waiting," Ella said.

"Oh, right. My secret. Well…" He took a deep breath. Whereas he'd planned on confessing something stupid—like he loved singing in the shower—something about the way she looked at him, the way her lips were half-parted, the way the flickering light was reflected in her eyes, made him say so much more. "Ell…"

"Yes?"

"My secret is that…" His pulse should've been racing, but instead, his heartbeat felt curiously steady and dull. Almost as if his sudden penchant for his neighbor might've been a surprise to his head, but his heart had known all along. "I'm…ah…afraid I'm starting to like you more than I should."

"Wh-what do you mean?" she asked. Had he only imagined her breath's slight hitch?

The boys' raucous cries and laughter faded as Jackson fumbled for the right words. He never should have confessed such a thing. He'd already firmly established in his head that Ell was off-limits. She was untouchable and—

And…laughing. Ella Garvey was laughing at him.

"What's so funny?" he demanded.

Leaning into him, mirroring his pose, she whispered, "What's funny is that your secret is the same as mine. I didn't want to come tonight because of your pending reunion with Julie. I, well…" Ducking her gaze, she admitted, "The last thing I wanted was to come between Dillon and the possibility of him getting his family back."

Settling against his chair, staring up at the evening's first stars, Jackson exhaled a long, slow breath.

"What's that mean?" she asked, voice a wobbly version of her usual in-control tone.

"Just that it's incredible to me that here we've lived so close to each other all these years—for the past two years have suffered through similar fates—yet only just now, when Julie finally gets her act together, do we actually talk."

"I know," she said with a nervous titter. "It's crazy. See why I didn't want to say anything?"

He nodded.

"Dad!" Dillon shouted. "Is dinner almost done?"

"Crap!" Jackson said under his breath. "I hope the potatoes aren't burned."

Ella giggled.

"Think that's funny, do you? Have you had a charred potato?"

"Too many times to count. I'm hopeless when it comes to barbecuing."

"In that case," he said with a wink on his way to the grill, "you should be in luck."

Luckily for all of them, Jackson was very good with a grill, and after Ella had settled Rose onto a makeshift quilt pallet for an after-dinner nap, they feasted on steak and loaded baked potatoes and the Caesar salad Ella and the boys had made. For dessert, they had brownies Ella had brought. They were sweet and chewy and as delicious as the company. It had been a long time since he and Dillon had laughed over a meal, but from here on out, Jackson vowed things were going to change. Whether he reunited with Julie was irrelevant. What truly mattered was that he make things right with his son. The way they used to be. Even if he never shared that kiss he craved with Ella, he owed her an incalculable amount of thanks for snapping him out of his funk. For reminding him he not only had a life to lead, but a rich, full life.

Tears stung his eyes, and he looked away from his guests and son.

"Yeah," Dillon said, continuing the story he'd been relating about what had happened that day in Mrs. Morgan's second-grade class, "and then when the rabbit got out, it pooped all over Bonnie Taylor's new shoes, and man, you should've heard her scream."

While Owen and Oliver hooted with laughter, Jackson and Ella shared a look. One that conveyed volumes without saying a word on the subject of how bizarre it was that nothing entertained the boys quite like the subject of fecal matter.

"Thank you," Ella said with a hug Jackson never wanted to end after they'd put away the leftovers and shared the work of the dishes. "It's been a really nice night."

"You're welcome, and I agree. When should we do it again?"

"Whoa," she said, palms pressed to his chest. "Slow down. I already told you that I have no intention of coming between you and Julie."

"Fair enough," he said with a formal bow. "But what if I told you that from the start, I wasn't as sure about Julie and I getting back together as Dillon has been?"

Jackson had expected her to be pleased with this news, but instead, she turned her back on him and headed into the entry hall where the boys had tucked Rose into her carrier.

"Ell?" he said, stepping behind her, not touching her, but surely close enough that she sensed his presence. "Did I say something to upset you?"

"No. Yes." Spinning to face him, she said quietly, so that only he could hear, "You have to know I always enjoy being with you. I consider Dillon as dear as my own son. But because of that, I have to—no, I *want* to—ensure he has every happiness he deserves. And if that means giving up on this…this curiosity we've developed for each other, then so be it."

"But—"

"Shhh…" Her back to the chattering boys, she shocked him by covering his mouth with her fingertips. "Promise me,

Jackson, that you'll at least give Julie a chance. Give your family a chance."

"Ell, I—"

"Promise, Jackson. I've been betrayed by someone I love. I won't do it to someone else." Her eyes were beseeching, her tone endearing, her conviction beyond admirable. As attracted to Ella as he was, he was that much more in awe. "Promise?"

Spirit-weary, Jackson gave her his word.

"WELL?" RACHEL ASKED in between patients the next day. She'd earlier admitted to badly craving a cigarette and was chewing her gum extra hard. "How was the big steak dinner?"

Ignoring her friend in favor of studying four-year-old Caitlin Marsh's chart, Ella simply said, "Fun. The night was fun."

"Just fun?"

"You sound disappointed." She did a quick scan of the patient's complaints. *Slight fever, sore throat, persistent cough.*

"Did he kiss you?"

"Rachel," Ella warned.

"Give me a break. I saw the way he looked at you the other day when he came in. Sure, at the moment, you're just in the exploratory phase of your relationship, but judging by how close the boys are—"

"Exploratory phase?"

Rachel shrugged. "I tape *Oprah*. But back to the topic at hand, did he?"

"Did he what?"

"Kiss you," her nurse said in a stage whisper. "I want details. Lots and lots of juicy, kissing-a-hunky-fireman details."

Carly, the resident insurance specialist, popped her head around her officer corner. "He *did* kiss her?"

"You know about this, too?" Ella asked.

"Everyone does," said Paige, the pint-size receptionist, on her way out of the break room. "Face it, we all lead frightfully dull lives. Lately, you're better than *The Young and the Restless*." She winked.

"Guys," Ella said, eyeing each and every one of them, "I know you mean well, but please, lay off. I'll be the first to admit, Jackson's a hunk, but he didn't kiss me, and never will. He's patching things up with his wife, and that's that." Pasting on a smile brighter than she felt, she added, "I'm happy for him and his son. You all should be, too."

Paige said, "Honey, that man's wife did him wrong. *Bad* wrong. You, on the other hand, have never hurt anyone or anything—except for that ant colony you annihilated under your crawl space last spring."

"Oh—and the squirrels in her attic." Rachel scratched her head. "And don't forget the opossum family in her garage."

"Great, I feel so much better knowing my dearest friends consider me a menace to nature—and, FYI, I live-trapped the opossums and the squirrels. Now, any chance of us seeing some patients?"

"Mmm…" Julie said with a firm hug. "I missed you."

Though Jackson returned the hug, he wished he could return the sentiments. It'd been barely over a week since her last visit, and truthfully, he wasn't sure he was ready for her to be back. But then Ella's words came to mind, along with the promise he'd made her.

…at least give Julie a chance. Give your family a chance.

"Mom!" Dillon raced down the stairs, tossing his arms around Julie's waist. "I'm so glad you're home."

The joy radiating from his son made Jackson feel like a

jerk. What was wrong with him that he couldn't get on board with the *Yay, Mom's back* parade?

"Come see my room," Dillon said, taking Julie by her hand. "I cleaned it just for you. And, look—" he puffed his chest "—I put on this icky shirt Grandma Franny gave me, even though I don't like it, because I know you do."

"You're a sweetheart," Julie said, ruffling his hair. "We'll have to take a picture of you wearing it, so she can see." Fran was Julie's mom and lived on an Arizona golf course. She also happened to have seriously disturbing taste in clothes— proven by Dillon's black-and-purple shirt with the dancing cows around the collar, sleeves and hem. "I'm sure she'll be very proud of how handsome you look."

Dillon made a face. "Do we have to take pictures? I don't want anyone else to see."

"Why?" she asked, kneeling to be at his eye level.

Dillon glanced at Jackson. "Dad…"

Clearing his throat, Dad came to the rescue. "Julie, in the time you've been gone, Dillon's grown quite a bit. Purple and black used to be his favorite colors, but he's a young man now, and—"

"Do you have to discredit me in front of our son?" Her eyes flashed fire.

"That's the last thing I'm trying to do," Jackson said, fingers at his throbbing temples. "I was only trying to make you see that—"

"Make me see? Like *I'm* the one with the problem? Well, for the record—"

"Stop!" Dillon had his hands over his ears. "Geez, Dad, I was so happy to have Mom home, why'd you have to go and ruin it by fighting? I'll wear the stupid shirt for the rest of my

Chapter Seven

"Hey, Jackson," Ella said early Friday night, glancing over her shoulder while removing the mixer from a batter-filled bowl. "Haven't seen you in a while. Where's your partner in crime?"

"Dillon?"

"Who else?" she asked with a laugh, telling herself it was exertion from baking six dozen cupcakes for the PTA bake sale that had her pulse racing, and not the sight of Jackson looking seriously yummy in faded jeans and a red T-shirt.

Dragging his finger through the chocolate batter, he crooned, "Mmm. That's good."

"It's also for the school. How long's it been since you last washed your hands?"

"At least four days," he said with a wink. "Sorry. Anyway, won't the oven's heat zap my cooties?"

"Yes," she said, "but, nevertheless, I pride myself on running a clean establishment." Releasing the beaters, she offered him one. He accepted and she took the other. "I love it when the boys are outside, and I get to do the licking."

"Me, too," he said. He'd gotten a dot of chocolate on the tip of his nose, and she automatically wiped it off.

"Sorry," she said when he dodged, caught unaware. Proving she'd had good reason to touch him, she held up her finger with the smudge of chocolate on it. "You looked like a bad boy with this on the tip of your nose."

"Thanks for rescuing my reputation," he said, catching hold of the base of her finger, bringing it toward his mouth where he proceeded to ever-so-lightly suck off the batter, never losing sight of her stare. "I'd hate for anyone—especially you—to think of me as bad."

Heart in her throat, it was all Ella could do to breathe, let alone think of a witty reply. Things like this didn't happen to her. *Ever.*

"Damn," he said, abruptly releasing her to cover his face with his hands.

"What's wrong?"

"That was seriously over the top, wasn't it? I mean, when Brad Pitt used it in his last action flick, it worked great for him, but—"

Ella kissed Jackson quiet. Then suddenly was mortified by her own behavior! What was she thinking? Apparently nothing, as she wanted to do it again.

"Wow," he said, a slow, sexy grin tugging the corners of his lips. "Your technique's way better than mine."

"No…" She shook her head. "I mean, yes, but that can't happen again. You're a married man."

"No, Ell, I'm not." Taking her hand, he twined her fingers with his, and she closed her eyes, inwardly sighing with guilty pleasure. It had been so long since she'd touched a man like this. Simply yet intimately. Emotion balled in her stomach. Hunger she'd thought extinct. Passion she'd all but abandoned. Hope, fear and the giddy, somersaulting excitement of a first crush.

"But you might as well be married," her rational side reasoned. "Julie's in town right now. In fact, why aren't you with her?"

"She took Dillon to get a haircut, then out for ice cream."

"Oh."

"They're having what her favorite parenting tome calls 'mother-son bonding.'"

"Oh."

"So, see?" he said, stroking her palm with his thumb, snaking forbidden heat through her limbs. "I'm totally *allowed* to be here with you."

"But—" For sanity's sake, she jerked her hand free, clutching it to her chest as if she'd been burned. "This is what I was talking about the other night at your house. You haven't even given Julie a chance. She's trying so hard to win Dillon back. And, presumably, you. Yet you're here with me. How will you even know if things might work out between you if you don't at least try? You promised me, Jackson, remember?"

He nodded. "Yeah, I remember. But when I'm with her, I'd rather forget. All we do is fight." His touch painfully tender, he skimmed his palm over the crown of her head. Ella wanted to relax into his touch, but couldn't—wouldn't, for it felt dangerously good. "When I'm with you, all I want to do is be with you more. You make me feel good inside. Happy. She makes me feel all tangled up and angry."

Ella's oven timer went off.

The annoying buzz woke Rose who'd been catnapping in a patch of early-evening sun in the baby swing Ella had bought her the previous day.

"I'll get her," Jackson said, already headed that way. "You get whatever smells so good in the oven."

The oven's heat did nothing to relieve Ella's blazing cheeks. Part of her was thrilled at Jackson's admission of not being as into his ex as she apparently was into him, but another part was mortified. Ella loved Dillon like one of her own sons. How could she deny him a mother for no better reason than to indulge her own selfish desires? The very notion went against everything she'd ever believed in. Her whole life had been centered around her children. Her career and, she'd believed—up until Todd's infidelity—her marriage.

Setting the cupcake pan on a cooling rack, she placed another already filled with colorful cups and white cake batter into the oven, then reset the timer.

She then made the mistake of looking Jackson's way. He held Rose in his arms; both were bathed in golden sunlight. Mouth dry, throat aching from wanting something she could never have and still live with herself, she turned to the counter.

There were cooled cupcakes to frost in Key Elementary School's red, white and blue colors. The task would make for a perfect distraction.

"Is it just me," Jackson said, unfortunately from close enough behind her that she felt his radiated heat, "or does this angel get cuter every day?"

"Jackson," she said in a voice scratchy from the effort of holding back tears. "I meant what I said about not being a party to ruining Dillon's life."

"Um, correct me if I'm wrong, but didn't Julie already do that? Why do either of us have to pay for her sins? All I'm suggesting is that you and I go on a few dates. Maybe even without four kids. Is that so scandalous?"

"No, but—" She dabbed a few squirts of red food coloring into a bowl of white frosting and stirred. Unfortunately, it only turned pink. She squirted in more and more, but the frosting still never got close to Key Cardinal Red. Why was it that her disastrous personal life felt the same? As though she could put as much effort as possible into forging a friendship with Jackson, but it didn't matter, as her conscience would never allow them to progress to a level anywhere near the perfection she sensed they might otherwise obtain.

Giving up, she dropped the spoon against the bowl's side, then rested her elbows on the counter and her forehead in her hands.

"Do you want me to leave?" Jackson asked, still behind her. He smelled of a hint of spicy aftershave, and Rose's pink baby lotion.

"Yes." *No!*

"All right. I have no intention of sticking around where I'm not wanted."

"It's not that," Ella said on the heels of a frustrated groan. Spinning to face him, she said, "I know what you mean—about being happy whenever you're around. There's something about you, maybe the fact that we shared similarly crappy marriages, that makes me feel I can trust you. But even beyond that, when we first learned the boys had run away, you radiated a quiet strength and determination to make everything okay that I've never seen in anyone else."

"I have." Free hand cupping her cheek, he said, "I've seen it in you. That's why we've got this connection. My grandmother used to call it a case of kindred spirits."

"That's all well and good," she said, "but is that the line you're going to feed Dillon when he asks why you're with me instead of his mother?"

SATURDAY AFTERNOON, while Julie had gone off in search of a restroom, Jackson stood in line with Dillon to buy corn dogs. They were spending the day at a neighboring town's annual arts and crafts fair, but so far, he and his son had seen far more food than art. The weather was fine with only a few high clouds and plenty of warm, but not yet hot, sun. A ragtime band played in a gazebo, lending a festive spirit to the bustling crowd.

"Having fun?" Jackson asked, moving up in line.

"Uh-huh." Dillon popped a gum bubble that stuck to his cheeks. In true kid form, he peeled it off, then crammed it back in his mouth. "This is the best day I've ever had in my *whooole* life."

Rubbing his son's shoulders, Jackson asked, "What about the time we went fishing in Colorado?"

"Nope. This is better."

"Why? I thought catching all those trout was pretty cool."

"It was," Dillon said, temporarily stepping out of line to spit his gum in the trash. "But Mom wasn't with us, so since she *is* here today, that makes it lots better."

"Oh." Jackson wished with every fiber of his being he felt the same. He supposed he'd been having an all right time, but Julie had worn high heels that kept getting stuck in the grass, and every five minutes she was stopping to slather sunscreen on Dillon's freckled nose.

"Whew," Julie said, teetering up beside them. "That was a long walk."

"Why don't you take off those shoes?"

"And go barefoot?" Her perfectly arched eyebrows raised. "Yesterday, I had a fifty-dollar pedicure."

"Just a suggestion," Jackson said with a shrug.

When it was their turn in line, Jackson and Dillon ordered corn dogs and lemonade while Julie got bottled water.

Thirty minutes later, the guys ordered funnel cake, and Julie guzzled more bottled water before whining about needing to make another trek to the bathroom.

An hour after that, it was caramel apples and Cokes. This time, Julie ate, but only a plain apple—oh, and of course, more bottled water.

A long time ago, Jackson had been a big fan of Julie's rail-thin body, but with the years, he'd packed on a few pounds, and felt comfortable with them. He'd tired of watching every little thing he ate, and though he tried to eat healthily, he didn't shy away from culinary fun. Years ago at a neighborhood block party, Julie had made a comment about how Ella had gotten fat. At the time, Jackson hadn't thought much about the statement, but now that he'd spent time with Ella, he saw her as fun-loving and full of energy and a seriously great cook. So what if she had a little junk in her trunk? He liked it—considered her damned sexy. More importantly, he liked her. He liked the way she seemed to enjoy every minute of her life.

"Dad?" Dillon asked in front of a pottery display.

"Yes?"

"When are you and Mom having the new wedding? I've gotta send out in-vo-tations."

Hands in his pockets, Jackson said, "The word is *invitations,* but you need to cool your jets. We haven't even decided if there's going to be another wedding."

"Why?"

Jackson wanted to refer to Julie for help, but she was haggling with the booth's owner over the price of a truly ugly brown vase.

"Bud," Jackson said with a sigh, "it's like this. Me and Mom don't always see eye to eye on things."

"What's that mean?"

Steeling his jaw, Jackson tried thinking of a kid-friendly explanation. "Basically, your mom and I are kind of like Owen and Oliver. Deep down, we love each other, but sometimes, we don't like each other."

"Oh." Lower lip trembling, Dillon looked Julie's way. "She's awfully pretty, though, right Dad?"

Jackson had once thought her the most beautiful woman in the world. But her leaving had shown him an ugly side of her he hadn't previously known. He'd been adult enough to understand her need for big-city career excitement, even though he damn sure hadn't liked it, but Dillon had been mighty confused. The kid had thought Julie was mad at him. Ridiculous, but how did you rationalize lofty career goals to a five-year-old?

"Isn't this gorgeous?" Julie asked, beaming, vase in hand. "I got the artist to come down to a hundred. I think that's a great deal, don't you?"

"If you're into that sort of thing."

"You don't like it?" She pouted. "I thought this would look great in your den."

"Um, sure," he said, taking the vase from her because it looked heavy. As an added plus, if he accidently tripped, he could be sure it broke.

"How was it?" Ella asked Jackson Sunday afternoon as they sat in Key Elementary's crowded gymnasium. Rose slept in her carrier on the seat to her left. In conjunction with the bake sale and a silent auction, the kids were performing a singing version of *Beauty and the Basketball-Playing Beast.*

"You mean this weekend?" he asked, breath warm on her cheek and neck. He smelled of one of the chocolate cupcakes he'd purchased. "With Julie?"

"Yes. What else would I be talking about?"

"Shhh!" scolded an angry parent from behind them.

"Sorry," Ella whispered back.

Taking a pen and notepad from her purse, she jotted: Did you have fun at the art fair? Are you back in love?

After reading her message, he shook his head.

Sorry, she wrote.

life if that's what Mom wants!" Crying, but doing an admirable job of trying to hide it, the kid raced up the stairs.

Shaking his head, Jackson wandered off to the kitchen. He needed a beer.

"You're just going to leave me?" Julie asked, close on his heels. "Don't you think we should talk?"

In front of the open fridge door, letting the cool air wash over him, Jackson said, "Why is it that back when you left me, I wanted to talk but you didn't? Now, all of a sudden, the tables are turned, but you can't stand it."

"I've apologized all I'm going to for leaving, Jackson. I've come to you, proverbial white flag waving, then you throw that crap in my face about Dillon having grown up. Don't you think I know that? Don't you think it's eating me up inside that my son is turning into a young man without me? I miss tucking him in, and reading to him and cooking his favorite meals. I miss folding his little shirts and undies and making sure he brushes his teeth."

"That's all well and good," Jackson said, "but do you miss anything about me? Do you get the fact that if you move in here, it's a package deal? You get me *and* Dillon, seeing how I'm not the leaving type."

She graced him with a slow, sarcastic round of applause Jackson guessed he had coming. "Great closing argument, I'm impressed. Been watching a lot of *Law & Order?*"

After grabbing his beer, he slammed the fridge door, rattling the condiments. "This bickering back and forth is getting us nowhere. Worse yet, it's hurting our son."

"Agreed." Hands on her hips, dressed in one of her signature black power suits and black patent-leather four-inch heels, she looked every bit the powerful lawyer, but nothing like a mother. Nothing like Ella. Not that he planned on making a play for Ella, because they'd already agreed that was a path neither wanted to go down. Still, no matter how much Julie professed to wanting to be a mother, Jackson feared she didn't have it in her. Just as she was instinctively a brilliant attorney, she was a lousy mom.

"Meatballs aren't stupid, Oliver. You are!"

"You are!" Oliver sassed back.

"Hush," Ella whispered loudly enough for both boys to hear and know exactly how serious she was. "Now, both of you get out your lists, and—" Her cell rang.

While she answered, out of the corner of her eye, she caught Oliver poking his brother's right side. With her free hand, she gently tugged a lock of hair on the back of his head, then shot him her best Evil-Mom stare. Anticipating a problem with one of her patients, she said, "This is Doctor Garvey."

"Hey, doc." It was Jackson. "Sorry to bug you, but a situation has cropped up that—"

"Wait—" she headed down the aisle from the boys "—let me guess. You suddenly find yourself starring in a wedding you didn't even know was happening?"

"How'd you guess?"

She laughed. "I'm making my apparently world-famous Swedish meatballs for your reception."

He groaned.

"Need moral support?"

"Bad. Would you mind?"

Her stomach fluttered at the prospect of spending more time with him. "Tell you what," she suggested, ignoring her warring conscience, "the boys and I were headed to Chunky's Pizza after picking up their baseball gear and Rose. Want to meet us in, like, thirty minutes?" Pulse racing, it occurred to her that she'd just asked him on a date. Way to go on steering clear of the man!

"Sounds super. Thanks. See you there."

She was just about to tell him he was most welcome, but he'd already disconnected. Which was probably a good thing, right? But if it was good, how come she was actually a little disappointed?

"Stop hitting me!" Owen cried.

She glanced up to find Oliver having batting practice on his brother.

"Oliver?" she scolded, taking the bat and setting it back into the display rack. "What's the matter with you? You know better than to hit your brother."

He touched his chin to his chest.

"Oh, no, you don't, mister. I want an answer. *Now.* What's bugging you?"

"Everything," he said.

"You're just mad 'cause Mom is making meatballs and you didn't get your way." Owen stuck out his tongue.

"Stop," she said to her youngest.

"Back to you, sweetie, what's got you feeling so mean?"

"Nothing."

She sighed. "Owen, hon, do me a favor and take Oliver's football gear back."

"No! I'm keeping it!" Oliver scrambled to grab the equipment, but Ella intervened, snatching it all, then handing it over to Owen. "Be sure this stuff gets put in the right spots, please."

"'Kay, Mom."

"Now," Ella said, kneeling in front of her scowling little man. "Aside from the fact that you're not playing football until at least junior high, what's the problem?"

"I already told you," he snapped. *"Nothing."*

She sighed. "We're not moving from this spot till you tell me what's going on behind those squinty little eyes."

"I don't have squinty eyes."

"No," she said with a half smile, cupping the side of his cheek. "Actually, you have very handsome eyes, but back to our original topic, you know I know when something's bugging you, so you might as well just tell me, or we won't have time for pizza."

For the longest while, he held tight to his silence, but then a few tears escaped, and he clambered into her outstretched arms.

"Sweetie," she crooned, "please, tell me—"

"It's not fair," he said on the heels of a hiccup.

"What's not?"

"How come Dillon's getting his mom back, but we can't have Daddy back? How come he has to be with that stupid Dawn? I hate her. She makes me wash my hands like every five seconds."

As much as Ella agreed with her son that Dawn tended to be somewhat of an obsessive-compulsive neat freak with a dash of germophobe thrown in for good measure, she held her tongue and aimed for the adult conversational course. "Here's the deal," she said, not quite sure where to begin. "Dillon's mom didn't leave because she stopped loving him or his dad, but because she, um—" *is beyond selfish* "—was really needed at her work. Now, I'm thinking maybe she's not as needed at her job, so she's got more time for Dillon and his dad."

"Did our dad leave because he *did* stop loving us?"

Wow! How did she answer that? She supposed as truthfully as she could without breaking her boy's heart.

Forcing a deep breath, she said, "Your dad loves you very much."

"Then how come he had another baby so he could forget us?"

"Sweetie, no. That's not why he had a baby with Dawn. Not because he didn't love you, but because he loves Dawn so much, that he wanted to—"

Arms crossed, Oliver snorted, then turned his back on her and walked away.

"Honey, come back. We're still talking."

"No, we're not. You're just lying, because you think it's what I want to hear. Face it, Mom, Dad's never coming home, and you don't even care!"

ELLA HAD RELAYED her latest kid trauma over two large pepperoni pizzas and a pitcher of Coke while the three boys were off playing in the kid-sized hamster habitats and ball pits. Afterwards Jackson conceded, "Okay, you win. That beats my wedding crap. What are you going to do?"

"Wish I knew." She sighed, nuzzling Rose's downy hair. "And speaking of other topics weighing me down, there's this cutie. Not that I don't love having her, but I'd forgotten how much work babies are."

"Want me to take her for a few days?"

"No. Thanks for the offer, though. I'll call Hank and see how he's coming along with finding her mother."

Jackson and Ella had been passing Rose back and forth, sharing their afternoons. When Dillon had come running in after school, breathless with excitement over the fact that Julie had told him they would soon be a family again, Jackson hadn't said a word to refute him. After all, why should he? Having Julie finally come to her senses and return home was what he'd prayed for, wasn't it? But despite countless nights' prayer, he was now consumed with doubts. What he'd felt for Julie last night when she'd been mothering Dillon was resentment. Downright anger for her audacity in believing he'd just roll over and take her back. Forgive and forget, as if she'd never hurt him and their son.

"We're some pair, huh?" He held out his arms for Rose. "My turn."

She handed the sleeping infant to him, and Jackson smiled when Rose snuggled into his chest.

"She likes you."

"Yeah, it's my animal magnetism."

"Probably more like your beating heart," she said with a grin, reaching for her drink.

"You're no doubt right, but can't you allow me at least a little daydreaming about my prowess with the ladies?"

"Correct me if I'm wrong, but you are the one whose ex wants to reconcile. I'd say that must prove something about your manliness."

"Ha, ha." He shot her a feeble grin. "Do you honestly think it's me Julie misses, or Dillon? Or, hell, for that matter, her master bath with a wall of windows?"

"Tough to say." Ella reached for a slice of pizza. "Maybe a combination of all three. The important thing to realize is that at least she's opened the door for a reconciliation. That's huge. If Dillon's already this excited, can you imagine how magical the day you and Julie remarry will be? With that end goal in mind, no matter what the initial catalyst, you can't lose."

Grabbing his fourth slice of cheesy heaven, Jackson grimaced. "That sounded more like a rah-rah speech for a football team than a lesson in love."

"Sorry," she said with one of her cute grins and a shrug. "Guess I spent too much time at the sporting goods store this afternoon. But think about it. In some ways, don't you think love resembles football? Sometimes you get the glory, but more often, as has been my luck of late, you end up flat on your back in the mud."

"Good point." After finishing their pizza in companionable silence, Jackson said, "For the past two years, I've been in the mud. Dillon, too. How do I know once domestic bliss wears off, Julie won't run again? Dillon couldn't take it."

Neither could I.

What he needed was a woman he could one-hundred-percent trust. A woman for whom family came first. Take Ella, for instance. She'd never leave her boys for some big city E.R. job. Even after discovering Todd's infidelity, she'd tried staying together with him for the kids. It had been Todd who'd ultimately left. Some in the neighborhood had secretly considered her a fool for giving Todd that second chance, but Jackson had considered her honorable. She'd taken her marriage vows as seriously as Jackson had taken his. Too bad the same couldn't have been said for their respective spouses.

"Honestly," Ella said, tracing the dancing bears on the plastic tablecloth, "all you have to go on is your gut instinct. Odds are Julie's sincere, but for your own sake—most especially, Dillon's—don't jump right back in to your relationship. Take it slow. Reacquaint yourself with the qualities you first loved about her. If it's meant to be, hopefully the rest will fall into place."

"Thanks," he said. "It means a lot that you care."

"Absolutely. Dillon's happiness is important."

The shine in her eyes told him she was sincere in wishing his son the best. But another part of him, the part more intrigued than ever by the creases at the corners of her lips, wondered… *What about my happiness, Ella?*

As soon as he'd thought the question, he dismissed it.

Of course, he'd be happy again with Julie, and, of course, Ella wished him the best. She was his friend. And as such, would no doubt have been shocked by the notion that he not only found her attractive, but that every time they were together like this, he found it harder to say goodbye.

"Not to butt into your parenting skills," she said, "but I think it'd be best if you have a frank talk with Dillon ASAP. Let him know that just because you and Julie are trying to work things out, there are no guarantees."

"Good idea." Especially since Jackson wasn't entirely sure he was even capable of forgiving Julie. "But you know what would be even better?"

"What's that?"

"Taking the boys for ice cream. What do you think?"

Frowning, she said, "I think you're trying to sabotage my diet."

"Is my evil plan working?"

"Sorry, but beyond walking off this pizza on my treadmill, the boys have homework, and I have more charts needing to be updated."

"Sure," he said, wishing his chest weren't tight with disappointment. "Another time. We are still on for steaks tomorrow night, though, right?"

"You know, I'd love to, but—"

"What's the matter?" he couldn't help but blurt. "Why am I suddenly getting the cold shoulder? Trying to avoid me?"

"No. It's just that—"

"Mo-om!" Owen, breathless, crashed to a halt in front of their table, giving it a large enough jolt to startle Rose, who started screaming.

"What's the matter?" Ella asked, reaching for the baby and soothing her with crooning and a few jiggles. Was it wrong for Jackson to wish she'd work her magic on *his* frazzled nerves?

"Oliver and Dillon are stuck!" The boy pointed to a sharp turn in the highest section of the hamster maze.

Jackson looked up only to groan.

Sure enough, there were the two boys, arms and legs intertwined, faces contorted in tears—silent through the clear orange plastic tube. The kids were more shaken up than in any danger, and if they'd both calmed enough to think about it, they could've easily worked themselves free.

Shaking her head, Ella said, "This job has *you* written all over it."

"And here I was just thinking you were better suited for such a tight space."

She smiled sweetly. "While I appreciate the vote of confidence in my tiny derriere, you *are* the fireman."

"Damn," he mumbled good-naturedly under his breath.

"Uh-oh…" Owen wagged his index finger. "You said a swearword. Mommy, you gonna put him in time-out?"

"Just this once, I'll let it slide." Hands on her hips, she turned her attention back to Jackson. "Well? Aren't you going to the rescue?"

"Under one condition."

"What's that?"

"You and the twins come for steak tomorrow."

"I already told you, I—"

"Mom, say yes, or Oliver and Dillon are gonna die."

Rolling her eyes at her son's theatrics, Ella stood firm. "I just don't think it's a good idea."

"Why?" Jackson pressed. "What could be wrong about a good meal shared with good friends?"

"Yeah, Mom," Owen said, looking back and forth between the two adults. "It sounds fun to me."

"Help!" Came a muffled cry from above.

"All right," Ella said with a sigh. "We'll be there, just please, get those two down from there, so I can give them a piece of my mind."

He shrugged.

A few dancing forest creatures skipped down the aisle, then the class beauties swirled across the stage in their bright-blue satin skirts. Ella sent up a silent prayer of thanks that she hadn't had girls, otherwise she'd have been stuck on the Sewing Committee instead of the Twig-Gathering Committee that had hot-glued sticks to brown sweatshirts.

"The boys look great," Jackson said. "You did a nice job on the costumes."

"Thanks."

"Shh!"

It took everything in Ella not to turn around and glare at the old biddy. After all, the music was loud enough she could hardly hear herself think. Instead, she wrote: When are you seeing Julie again?

He took the pen and paper, and in the process, brushed his hand against hers. She ignored pleasurable sparks, telling herself it must be a chill causing goose bumps on her forearms. He scribbled: She'll be back next weekend.

Ella snagged the paper back and penned: That'll be nice for Dillon.

The look he returned her said, yes, it would be nice for his son, but Jackson wasn't all that excited. A part of Ella was thrilled at this notion that he didn't want to be with Julie, but the part of her who loved Dillon mourned. If she really wanted to help the boy get his family back, clearly, she'd have to try harder to steer clear of his father.

Ella took the pad and pen and shoved them into her purse. Passing notes like fourth-graders would not help her cause. Neither would sitting crammed alongside Jackson in a too-small folding chair, the right side of her body tingling from shoulder to thigh where they touched.

HER GAMBLE had paid off. They were there. Knowing the twins attended Key Elementary, she'd begged off early from work at the House of Fabric, then hustled down to the school. She'd been grateful to Larissa Chambers, whose daughter was in the same grade as Owen and Oliver, for telling her about the program.

She couldn't see her baby from the gym's edge, so she worked up all of her courage and actually sat in the row behind Ella Garvey and Jackson Tate. Every time Ella shifted, she had an amazing view inside her baby's fancy new carrier. She'd gotten so big. Her coloring was so pretty, and her hair had even grown long enough that Ella had put a tiny red bow in it that matched her baby's red sailor dress and shoes.

The longing to grab her baby girl was so great, it squeezed her chest. It had been forever since she'd seen her. But she couldn't very well just drop by Ella's house. If her grandmother or daddy ever found out about her pregnancy, she wouldn't live through the shame. They were a highly religious family—real regular churchgoers—and none of their congregation would understand.

She'd tried talking to Wes—just talking to him—but he wanted nothing to do with her now that he was going out with Pauline. Just as well, she supposed. Fooling around with him once had been the worst mistake of her life. She sure didn't need to go doing it again.

More than anything, she wished she could find a better job, save some money and steal back her baby and just run away. But deep in her heart, she knew what was best for her baby was the family she was currently with.

It hurt her that her child wouldn't grow up with a daddy, but she would have great older brothers to watch out for her and make sure no one picked on her in school. Although, the way Ella and Jackson were carrying on, who knew? Maybe some day they'd end up together, and her baby girl would have a whole family to love.

FINALLY, THE PROGRAM ENDED. The boys had all looked adorable and had done Oscar-worthy performances, but never had Ella been so glad to rise from her seat in a standing ovation, then beat a hasty retreat from the crowded gym.

Rose was awake, and Jackson scooped her from her carrier, holding her in the crook of one arm, and the carrier with his other.

"Want me to get that?" Ella asked.

"Nope. I've got it." He kissed Rose's cheek, and Ella could've sworn the baby smiled.

"Was that a grin?" she asked Rose in a silly voice, tickling her tummy.

"I think it was," Jackson said in a goofy falsetto, jigging the baby with each word.

"It's too early," Ella pointed out. "But she is obviously quite advanced for her age."

"And why wouldn't she be?" Jackson stated. "With us as temporary parents, her brilliance is a no-brainer."

"Didn't we do good, Mommy?" Owen asked, crushing Ella in an ambush hug.

"You were amazing," she said, laughing from the surprise of his whirlwind appearance.

"You sure did," Jackson echoed. "Where are Dillon and Oliver?"

"Oliver's talking to Harriet Grange—" he made a face as if this was worse than eating slugs "—and Dillon's having a stick war with Michael and Billy."

"There's my boy. Good job." Todd approached, Dawn in

tow. "Jackson," Todd said, extending his hand for him to shake, then laughingly pulling back upon realizing the man had no free hands. "Looks like you could use our nanny."

"I'm good," Jackson said.

"Having a nanny's better," Todd said with a wink, elbowing his petite new bride.

Dawn sighed. "You can't offer Eloise around like a platter of deviled eggs."

"Did I say I was?" Todd asked. Attention back to Owen, he said, "How about heading out with me and Dawn for burgers?"

"Really?" Owen asked with an excited hop. "I'll go get Oliver."

"Thanks for asking me first, Todd." Ella hated exposing her snippy side to Jackson, but honestly, when Todd showed up out of the blue, whisking the boys off for adventure, it was annoying.

"Don't cop an attitude, Ella. You know my schedule's nuts this time of year. This was the only free afternoon I've had all week."

"It's fine," she said, arms crossed. "Just have them home by eight or so. It's a school night."

By the time Ella got the boys settled with Todd, the crowd had thinned. Jackson stood waiting for her in a corner of the cafeteria, munching an oatmeal cookie. Rose was eyeballing her toes in her carrier at his feet.

"These are good," he said. "Who made them?"

"Angie Crawford. She's one of Dillon's homeroom moms."

"I'm marrying her," he said with charming wink, while slipping his arm around Ella's shoulders. For a split second, she savored his touch, then her least favorite busybody mom, Marcia Jenkins, strolled by.

"Ella," she said with an ultrafake smile. "I didn't know you and Jackson were an item."

"Actually," Ella said, "we're just—"

"Keeping our relationship under wraps for now," Jackson said in a bold whisper. Tugging her closer, he kissed her cheek. "But trust me, the minute we have something official to announce, we'll write it up for your newsletter."

"That would be wonderful," Marcia said, eyeing Rose. "Is this the infant your boys found?"

"Actually," Jackson said, "we left that baby at home. This one's our secret love child."

"Jackson." Ella gave him a swat. "He's kidding," she said to Marcia.

Eyebrows raised, Marcia pursed her lips, then shook her head and walked off.

"What'd you do that for?" Ella demanded.

"I can't stand the woman. Ever since she's started yelling at me for not dropping Dillon in the proper loading and unloading zones, I've had it out for her. That was fun."

"Still, you should've taken the moral high road."

"Relax," Jackson said, rubbing her left shoulder. "Marcia's probably got a love child, too. And if she doesn't, then she's just jealous of ours."

"Stop." Ella pretended to scold, a half smile tugging her lips.

"I won't stop," he said in a whisper all hot and breathy in her ear. "And just think, if you'd come to your senses and give me a chance, not only would we share our love child, but our other kids, as well." He winked. "You've always said you practically consider Dillon to be your own son."

"Yeah, but there's a big difference between *practically*

thinking of him in terms of being mine, and me actually being his mom. In fact—"

"Dad?" the boy in question said from behind them, expression crestfallen. "Is that true? Is Ms. Garvey really going to be my mom?"

Chapter Eight

"I hate you!" Dillon cried. "Both of you!" After giving both grown-ups hard stares, the boy took off running through the cafeteria and into the school lobby.

"That could've gone better," Jackson said, already chasing down his son. To Ella, who looked mortified by other moms' stares, he called over his shoulder, "Wait here."

Jackson finally tracked Dillon down on the playground. He was pumping back and forth in a swing, going higher than Jackson had ever seen him before.

"How about slowing down?" he asked.

"No!" Dillon sassed.

Not accustomed to his son back-talking, Jackson wasn't sure whether to yank him off the swing and ground him, or give him a hug. Of all times for him to have popped up out of nowhere. He and Ella had just been goofing around. What was the big deal? "Come on, bud. Let's talk."

"I already said, no! Just as soon as I'm done swingin', I'm runnin' away!"

That's it…

Teeth gritted against saying something he might later regret, Jackson timed Dillon's rise and fall, then snagged the swing's rusty chain.

"Hey! What'd you do that for?"

"Because we need to talk about what you *think* you heard."

"You said Ms. Garvey is gonna be my mom, but I already have a mom, and *she* loves me. I don't want another mom."

"First off…" Jackson said, lifting Dillon into his arms and carrying him to a bench nestled beneath a tall maple. On a sunny day, the tree made for nice shade, but today, the sky was gray. "Ella loves you, too. You're like family to her, only in an extra-special way because she chooses to include you in her life."

"I don't care. I hate her." Arms crossed, Dillon bowed his head.

"I happen to like her. A lot. But not nearly enough to officially make her your mom."

"Then why'd you say she was going to be my mother?"

Sighing and raking his hand through his hair, Jackson said, "You like jokes, right?"

"Duh."

"Well, what you heard was a joke. You know how I don't really get along with Heather Jenkins's mom?"

"Yeah. She's really strict about how many juice boxes we get, and her perfume smells like Grandma Franny's stinky hairspray."

Chuckling, Jackson had to agree. "Right. So, Heather's mom was being snooty about Rose, and it made me mad— just like when she yells at me about where to drop you off in the mornings."

"You *are* a bad mom when it comes to school drop-off, Dad."

"True," Jackson said, laughing again, "but back to what I was talking about—the first part of my joke was that I told Heather's mom that Rose was, um, Ella's and my baby."

"But, Dad…" Dillon looked up, eyes wide enough that Jackson feared his son might be doing the math on the mechanics of how babies were made. The adding up of what he and Ella would've had to do. The very thought raised Jackson's core temp a good twenty degrees. "Me and Owen and Oliver found her fair and square."

Whew. At least he was temporarily out of the woods on the whole How-Babies-Are-Made speech. "You did find her. That's why what I said was a joke. What you heard, about Ella being your mother, was me getting in trouble. Ella was scolding me for even teasing about something like that. Something else you need to know, is that you are very important to her. She would never do anything to hurt you. My joke was a bad one. Inappropriate, and I'm sorry that for even a little bit, I hurt you." Settling his arm around his son's sagging shoulders, he gave him a hug. Kissed the top of his head. "I love you."

"Love you, too, Dad, but please don't do that again."

"What? Joke about Rose?"

"No." Dillon pulled away, turning sideways on the bench. "Don't say stuff about you and Ms. Garvey—" he blanched "—doin' it. Mom wouldn't like that." So much for Jackson being in the clear on that speech.

"When you guys are getting married again, that's not very funny."

Rubbing his forehead, Jackson couldn't quite figure how to tackle this latest cog in his struggle to become a better dad. How did he explain to his seven-year-old son that he wasn't enthusiastic about the whole Let's-Get-Remarried plan? A year ago, hell, maybe even a month ago, he might've thought differently, but since connecting with Ella, he'd found himself torn. It wasn't as if he had any grand intentions toward his comely neighbor. Just the very fact that he was intrigued by her told him he wasn't in the right mindset to embark on a second go-around with the woman who'd broken his heart.

"Dad?" Dillon asked. "You and Mom *are* getting married again, right?"

Inwardly groaning, Jackson struggled for the right words.

"Dad? *Please* say you're getting married again." Dillon's voice cracked, and his eyes shone with unshed tears. The boy had never cried easily. Maybe it was an inherited trait from Julie, but even when he'd broken his arm falling out of a backyard tree, he hadn't dropped so much as a tear. To see him now on the verge—just as he was when Jackson and Julie argued—spoke volumes on how much he was counting on his family getting back together. *"Please."*

"Bud…" Jackson looked to the sky. Divine intervention would be nice. Unfortunately, about the only help in sight was a robin hopping beneath the slide. "I'm trying, okay? But, since your mom left, I don't feel the same about her as I used to."

"You don't love her anymore? The other day you said you did."

"I do love her," Jackson said with an exasperated sigh. "Without her, I wouldn't have you, but it's more complicated than that."

"How?" Kicking at the ground, Dillon said, "If you love her, you love her. She's pretty and nice and smells like flowers. All you gotta do is get married again, and she'll live with us forever. You're just not trying hard enough."

Right. Only with Julie, *forever* didn't have the same meaning as it did with the rest of the world.

"Please, Dad." Dillon's tears spilled, ripping Jackson in two.

More than anything, he loved his son. He used to feel that way about Julie, too. Maybe Dillon was right, and all he had to do was try harder to remember the good times and forget the bad.

But then there was Ella. Whenever he was around her, he felt better. Filled with hope. Actually excited about living in a way he hadn't been in a long time. He didn't have to *try* wanting to be with her. He just did. Being with Ella felt as natural as breathing.

He glanced up to see her heading across the playground, Rose in her arms. She must've left the carrier inside. In a red sundress with small blue polka dots, she'd never looked better. Only the worried crease between her eyebrows as she neared showed her to be anything other than relaxed.

"Hey, guys," she said, voice breezy. "We were getting worried about you."

"We're fine," Dillon snapped.

"Knock it off," Jackson said, nudging his son's ribs.

"Dillon," Ella said, pausing in front of the bench. Rose had grabbed hold of a chunk of her hair. "How long have you known me?"

"I dunno," he mumbled, head bowed.

"Like a million years?" she prompted.

"I guess."

"In those million years, have I ever done anything to hurt you?"

He shook his head.

"Why do you think I would do something now?"

"Because you want to steal my dad from my mom?"

Jackson winced at the pain and shock on Ella's features. She didn't deserve this, and the only reason she was having to go through it was because of him and his big mouth.

"Actually," Jackson said, "nobody has wished more for me to patch things up with your mom than Ella. She loves you, Dillon, and wants you to be happy. Especially if that means you getting to be back with your mom."

"Oh." The boy still held his head down.

"Do you think it might be nice for you to apologize to Ella?"

He shrugged.

"No apology necessary, sweetie," Ella said. "I just want us to keep on being friends."

Jumping up from the bench, Dillon tossed his arms around her waist for a teary hug.

"WHAT WERE YOU THINKING?" At seven that night, Ella lashed into Jackson the second Dillon dashed out the back door to join Owen and Oliver in their fort. Rose was content in her swing and Ella had just about finished preparing a simple meal of pork chops, mashed potatoes and salads when Jackson and Dillon had shown up at her front door. Supposedly, Dillon had wanted to play with the twins, but she suspected his father had had more to do with the impromptu appearance. "I told you not to mess with Marcia Jenkins, and look what happened. Dillon hates me. Practically accused me of being a home wrecker, when all along, I—"

Jackson stopped her rant by cupping her face with his hands, then wreathing her in the heat of a spellbinding kiss.

Back to her senses, she pushed him away. "What'd you do that for? What if Dillon had seen?"

"I know he couldn't, because from here I have a clear shot of the backyard. I just—" He put his hand to his suddenly throbbing forehead. "You sounded so upset. I didn't know any other way to make you feel better."

She cocked one eyebrow. "Think that highly of yourself, do you?"

"Work with me, here, will you? I need your help."

Turning her back on him to resume making the salads, she laughed. "Oh, you need help all right, but I'm not volunteering. This situation has *powder keg* written all over it."

"How so?" he asked, snatching a cherry tomato. "We had a

nice talk back at school, you two seem back on good terms. Next time Julie's in town, I fully intend to take a fresh perspective. But until then, I refuse to act as if I don't care about you."

Exasperated, she chopped down hard on a cucumber and ended up slicing her finger. Yelping in pain, she tugged a paper towel from the under-cabinet holder, then wrapped it around her bleeding wound.

"Let me see," Jackson said, crowding her personal space, fogging her mind by taking her injured hand. "It looks bad. Think you need stitches?"

"No. Just a minute of direct pressure."

"Allow me." He held the makeshift bandage just right, not too hard to hurt, but firm enough to do the job. In the process, his proximity dulled her senses and made her want to spend the rest of the night standing alongside him. Resting her forehead against his chest, she exhaled.

"What was that about?" he asked, stroking her hair.

"This situation. It's impossible. From what you've told me, it's a lose-lose for everyone but Dillon. Oh—and Julie."

Looking at her finger, Jackson said, "It's stopped bleeding. Got a Band-Aid?"

"Third drawer on the left," she said, pointing to the side of the stove. "SpongeBob, please. The antibiotic ointment is in there, too."

"Yes, ma'am." In no time, he was back, dabbing the ointment on her cut, then easing the bandage around her finger, kissing the tip. "Better?"

She nodded.

"I'm sorry."

"It wasn't your fault. I was the one with the knife." She tossed the knife in the sink, then grabbed a fresh one from a drawer before resuming her task.

"I'm not talking about your gash. I feel bad about messing with Marcia. I feel worse about the things Dillon said. He didn't mean them, you know. He's just got this image of Julie moving back home and us all living happily ever after. He viewed you as a threat to that, and snapped."

"I get that," she said, now dicing a tomato, "but that doesn't change the fact that exactly what he's afraid of is true. I am in the way of you and Julie growing closer."

Now it was his turn to cock an eyebrow. "Think that highly of yourself, do you?"

"OUR MOM WOULD *sooo* not marry your dad," Oliver said, pointing his wooden sword in Dillon's direction.

"Don't get all mad with me," Dillon said, pointing his plastic sword at Oliver. "I'm just telling you what I heard."

"Our mom doesn't even like boys," Owen said, munching the oatmeal cookies he'd smuggled into the clubhouse. "Except for us. She loves us."

"Yeah, she loves *us*." Oliver leaped from the cooler he'd been standing on to the old recliner their mom had let them have. The chair bounced a little, but didn't break.

"My mom loves me," Dillon said.

"Did we say she didn't?" Man, Oliver wanted to stab Dillon with his sword for saying those things about his mom. No way would she ever cheat on him and Owen with Mr. Tate. He was cool and all, but not anywhere near cool enough to be kissing his mom. Only his dad was allowed to do that, and just as soon as he dumped Dawn and their bad kid, Oliver knew he'd be coming home. How? Because if Dillon's mom loved him enough to marry his dad again, then Oliver's dad for sure loved him and his brother enough to remarry his mom.

"WHOA," RACHEL SAID Monday morning during a patient lull. She and Ella sat on top of the picnic table placed out back of the clinic for use as an alternate break room on sunny days. "Sounds like you had a seriously crappy weekend."

"I've had better," Ella said, tipping her face back to drink in the sun. "The worst of it wasn't Dillon screaming he hated me, but knowing the look of betrayal in his eyes was because of me."

"Stop." Rachel, for once gum-free, rubbed Ella's back. "You can't help the fact that Jackson's over his ex any more than you can control your gorgeous smile that's obviously making him want you."

Ella snorted. "Jackson Tate doesn't know what he wants. I'll bet if Julie turned on her charm, she'd have him back on board in no time."

"I think you're underestimating *your* charms. What you need is a weekend away from the kids. Just you and Jackson, figuring out if there's more here than just your garden-variety flirtation."

Sighing, Ella climbed off the table to pace. "I already told you, I'm not figuring out anything in regard to Jackson. He's off-limits. If Dillon's reaction to a joke was that dramatic, think how he'd feel knowing Jackson and I have kissed."

"Ah-hah!" Rachel said with a triumphant smile. "So you *have* macked on the hunky fireman."

Ella rolled her eyes.

The office's back door creaked open, and Paige poked her head out. "Ella! Hank's on the phone for you."

Rachel asked, "Think he's got news about Rose's mom?"

Making a face, Ella said, "Is it wrong that I've grown so attached to her that I almost hope not?"

Rachel patted her back. "Understandable, considering what a cutie she is."

"Thanks." Ella blew her friend a kiss before dashing inside. "Hey, Hank," she said a minute later on her office extension. "What'd you find out?"

"Unfortunately," he said in his gravel-toned baritone, "not a whole lot. We had a couple of good leads, checking out high-school girls who'd dropped out midsemester, but none panned out. The school route would've been easiest. Now, we're branching out to neighboring high schools and the community at large, but it's going to take time. You hanging in, or want me to call Child Protective Services?"

"I'm good," she said, her stomach in knots at the mere thought of this innocent child being lost in government red tape. "Just keep looking, and let me know what you find."

"WHAT'RE YOU DOING?" On the front porch Wednesday morning, Ella yawned, then gripped her fuzzy pink robe tighter.

"What's it look like I'm doing?"

"Fixing my screen door."

"Ding, ding, ding. Give that lady a prize." He'd set up sawhorses, rested the door on edge across them and now used a planer to strip part of the wood from the bottom where it stuck. Even at seven, the day already promised to be muggy, and Jackson's white T-shirt clung to his back. As he worked the planer, his biceps bulged, filling Ella's belly with all manner of forbidden fires.

"Why are you fixing my screen door?" *Making me even crazier wanting you? Ruining my whole day with the image of your muscles that'll be superimposed over every patient's chart?*

"Because it needs fixing."

"Oh." The grin he shot her way was lethal—at least in

regard to her willpower. Honestly, the man was criminally good-looking. "Your door does, too."

"Already did it," he said with a masculine grunt.

"This morning?" Impressive. Especially since she'd had a tough time even getting out of bed.

"Yep."

"What's got you so industrious?"

"Excess energy."

"Interesting," she said, perching on the porch rail, struggling to keep the halves of her robe together. "Care to expound on the subject?"

He eyed her strangely.

"*That* kind of energy?" Heat rose in her cheeks.

"Get your mind out of the gutter, woman. I had things on my mind."

"Like what?" she asked, praying his answer was nice and dull.

"Women. Why is it when you want one, you can't find one, then when you're not looking, you end up with three?" He stepped up his pace.

"Correct me if I'm wrong," she said, only partially relieved his answer wasn't risqué, "but don't you only have one woman? Your wife?"

"My *ex*-wife. Then there's Rose, who, after you told me about Hank's call, I worry might be living with you till she's eighteen considering the speed of his investigative skills. Then, there's you." He punctuated his last statement by melting her with a heated stare. "And while technically, no, you're not yet mine, the more I'm with you, the more I like you. A problem, considering my son's stance on the matter."

"Speaking of Dillon, where is he?" She hoped Jackson wouldn't notice the change of subject. True, she did wonder where he'd stashed his boy, but she also had no desire to talk about the fact that the more she was around Jackson, the more she wanted to explore. His pecs. His abs. His scrumptious kisses…

"Dillon is gobbling my mother's pancakes. Wednesdays she comes over to do laundry."

"Nice. Send her my way when she gets done."

Quiet for a second, Jackson seemed to be searching for his next words. "This may sound mean, but sometimes I wish Mom would butt out. I know she means well, but I'm pushing forty and know how to do my own laundry."

"Did you ever think caring for you makes her feel good? Needed? Like she couldn't help you fix your marriage, but she can make sure you and Dillon eat great and have clean socks and undies?"

"Thanks," he said with a deep sigh. "Now, I not only sound mean, but I feel mean."

"You're not mean," she said, fighting the urge to go to him and slip her arms around him for a strictly comforting hug. "Just too proud for your own good."

"How's that?" He'd put down the planer to aim a dirty look her way.

"I'm just theorizing here," she said with a smile, "but I've got you pegged for the superhero type who feels like he can do anything and everything himself. You don't call plumbers or electricians, and having your mom taking care of you like she did in fourth grade makes you feel inadequate as a man."

His eyes got all squinty and a muscle worked in jaw. Oops. Direct hit to the male ego?

Chapter Nine

"I'm sorry." Ella did go to him, but stopped short of giving him that hug. "I'm jealous. My mom's too busy with her clubs even to think of helping me around the house."

"I've gotta go. I'll finish up later."

"Jackson," she said softly, just this once touching him because he obviously needed consoling. She started by skimming his back, then eased her hands around his waist, resting her cheek between his shoulder blades. "I really am sorry if I hit a nerve. What can I say? I aced all my psych classes."

"Then you must've cheated, because none of that crap you just spouted was true." Spinning to face her, he said, "Just because my mom does a few loads of clothes for me doesn't make me less a man."

"Of course, it doesn't. Isn't that what I just said?"

He started off the porch, but she snagged his arm. "Please, don't leave. At least stay and have a quick coffee." *Don't make me worry all day about having royally ticked off my best friend.* How their friendship had come about so quickly, she couldn't fathom. But now that she had Jackson in her life, she didn't want him to go.

That muscle kept ticking in his jaw. Medical books had

taught her a ticking nerve was a sign of pent-up stress being released. Technically, it was a good thing. Healthy. However, knowing she was the cause of his stress sucked.

"I guess I could have coffee," he grumbled. "But no more talk about my mother."

"Agreed."

"Or Julie."

He didn't have to twist her arm on that one.

"Mr. Tate, can you please pass the sugar?" Owen held out his chubby fingers, impatiently pinching.

"Here you go, but don't you think you've got enough?" The kid had already doused his Corn Flakes with three or four teaspoons.

"Nope," Owen said through a mouthful of cereal, dribbling milk down his chin.

Jackson passed him a napkin.

"Thanks."

Oliver slid into the vacant seat beside his brother. "How come you're here?" he asked their guest.

Jackson cringed. At the moment, seeing how Ella had abandoned him with her young—including Rose who wasn't too happy about being in her swing—he was asking himself the same question. How long did it take a woman to grab a so-called quick shower? "I was fixing the screen door, but your mom asked me in for coffee."

"I thought you were getting married," Oliver asked, pouring so much milk in his cereal bowl that it sloshed over the side.

Jackson dabbed the mess with a handful of napkins he'd grabbed from a holder in the table's center. "Isn't it time for you two to head off to school?"

"The carpool doesn't come for another five minutes," Owen informed him.

"Yeah," Oliver said, digging into his cereal with the spoon in his left hand and scooping on sugar with his right. "So? Are you getting married?"

"I'm...ah...not sure," Jackson said, telling the truth, eyeing his lukewarm coffee.

"Dillon says you are."

Dillon has a big mouth. "Tell you what, soon as I find out if I'm getting married, or not, I'll let you know."

"If you are getting married," Owen said, drinking his leftover milk from the side of his bowl, "how come you're all the time hanging around our mom?"

"Does it bother you that I'm here?"

Rose had transitioned from fitful complaining to a full wail.

Jackson went to her, gingerly lifting her from the swing, then settling her into his arms.

"Doesn't bother me," Owen said. "I like you. But Oliver says you're trying to steal our mom from our dad."

Resting his chin atop the baby's head—she was finally quieting down—Jackson sighed. Looked like it was going to be one of those days.

"I never said that," Oliver argued.

"Did, too. While we were brushin' our teeth last night, you said you wished Mr. Tate would go ahead and get married so he'd quit stealing Mom from Dad."

"Did not!" Oliver was on his feet, fists clenched. "Take it back!"

Owen stuck out his tongue.

"I hate you!" Oliver hollered. "I wish Mom would've never let you out of her belly!"

"Whoa, guys," Jackson said, rising to referee, not to

mention get Rose above the scuffle. He'd worried the raised voices would upset her, but judging by her wide-eyed stare, she was intrigued. "That's enough."

"I *do* hate him," Oliver mumbled.

"I hate you," Owen said. "Dad does, too, or he never would've left!"

Ouch. Talk about hitting below the belt. Jackson had forgotten how cruel kids could be.

The boys went from verbal missiles to kicking and fists.

"Ella!" Jackson bellowed, doing his damnedest to break the kids apart while keeping Rose safe.

"What's the matt—Owen! Oliver! Knock it off!"

"He started it," Owen said, huffing and out of breath.

"He's lying," Oliver said, casting his twin a glare. "And anyway, if he has to keep living here, I'm running away."

Sighing, Ella put her hands over her eyes and shook her head. She'd changed from her robe into tan slacks and a crisp white blouse, over which she wore a white lab coat with *Dr. Ella Garvey* embroidered in cursive on the pocket. Sometimes Jackson forgot how accomplished she was. There was no way she had time for kid wars.

From outside came the double honk of Mindy Ford's mom's minivan. He knew, because Dillon was in the same three-week-rotation carpool.

"Both of you grab your lunches and backpacks, and get outside." Hands on her hips, she added, "Don't think we're not going to talk about this when you get home."

"Bye, Mommy," Owen said, sneaking in a hug on his way past. "I'm sorry."

"Suck-up," Oliver mumbled, hot on his twin's heels.

"That was fun," Ella said after both boys had left the house,

Oliver slamming the door. "Bet that's the last time you show up for coffee over here."

He winced. "Are your mornings always this much excitement?"

"Usually. What brought all of this on?"

Jackson, Rose still in his arms, sat at the kitchen table. "Cliff's Notes version, Oliver asked when I was getting married. Fights ensued when Owen offered the fact that Oliver said I was trying to steal you from their dad. Oliver vehemently denied ever having said this, at which point, the bickering turned even uglier when Owen suggested Todd hated Oliver, which was why he left."

"Sweet little Owen said that?" Ella, gaping, took the chair beside him.

Jackson laughed. "'Sweet little Owen' has one helluva forked tongue."

"Sorry you had to deal with that," Ella said, holding Rose's tiny hand. "Remember when our boys used to be adorable like this? Never sassy. Worst thing they ever did was get you out of bed for a late-night feeding, but then they were so angelic to look at, you didn't even mind."

"What're we going to do?"

"We?" Ella landed a pointed stare right at him. "You're the one who's supposed to be getting married. I figure once you and Julie are rehitched, my two guys will magically become best friends."

At that, Jackson snorted. "Seen any donkeys flying lately?"

"Stranger things could happen," she said with a warm smile, taking Rose from his arms. "After all, who would've thought we'd end up with you?" She'd directed that last part toward the baby, kissing her cheek.

"Given the stress level around our homes lately, will you be sorry to see her go?"

"Yes," she said, drawing in her lower lip. "I'm pretty attached to her. I couldn't bear seeing her living with just anyone."

"I agree." He stared out the windows into the backyard, struggling for his next words. "Ell?"

"Hmm?" she asked, sipping her coffee.

"I need to apologize."

"For what? This is cold," she said, rising with her mug. "I'm dumping mine out and starting over. Want some?"

"No, thanks." What he had to say was hard enough without additional caffeine. When she'd returned from her mission, he took a deep breath. "Until witnessing that fight between your boys, I hadn't realized how much my rocky marriage has affected your usually serene life. For that, I'm sorry."

"Hush," she said, sipping the steaming, fragrant brew. "Oliver hasn't stopped being mad at Todd and me since the divorce. He's just been on hiatus. His anger has nothing to do with you. Owen grabs every chance he can to dig at his brother, so voilà, you have the perfect storm of kid angst."

"Yeah, but…" He put his free hand over hers. Was it the heat from her mug that had him humming with attraction, or Ella herself? Trying to get back on track, he cleared his throat. "Before Dillon started in with this whole remarriage thing, then telling your boys that I'm going to be their dad, all of your problems were at least on a nice low simmer instead of boiling over like they are now."

"Just think how boring that would be." She dazzled him with a wink and swift smile. Gripping his hand firmly, making him feel disturbingly whole when he wasn't supposed to feel anything for her other than nice, safe platonic friendship, she said, "I'm not sure how, but somehow we'll get you through this. You and Julie will finally patch things up. Dillon will be thrilled. My boys will finally get it through their thick skulls that Todd took off for greener, younger, thinner pastures because he's a cheating, lowlife bastard scum, and we'll all live happily ever after."

Earlier, they'd talked about donkeys flying? Ha. Jackson strongly suspected that in order for him to be happily married to Julie again, pigs would have to fly, as well. Not wanting to leave her or Rose, he asked out of the blue, "Do you really have to go in to the clinic today?"

"I really do." Grimacing, she glanced at her pink Minnie Mouse watch. "In fact, I'm already late."

"Can't you call in sick?"

Grinning, she tweaked his nose. "If I called in sick, then who would treat all of my sick patients?"

"ALL RIGHT, GUYS," Ella said that evening after dinner and before a dessert of pound cake and strawberries with whipped cream—the diet wasn't going so well! "Now that you've both had a chance to cool off, I want each of you to tell me what's going through your heads to have said such horrible things to each other this morning."

Oliver crossed his arms.

"Owen?" she prompted, looking to her youngest. "Do you have anything to say on the matter?"

He crossed his arms and stuck out his tongue at his twin.

"Okay," she said with a deep sigh. "This is going great. I guess I'll talk and you guys are going to listen."

Both boys stared hard at their empty dinner plates.

"Owen, Jackson told me what you said to Oliver about your father leaving because he hated him. That's one of the cruelest, nastiest, not to mention most false things you've ever said. I'm ashamed of you. You don't have to like your brother, but you *will* respect him, and what you said wasn't only disrespectful but mean. I thought you had a bigger heart than that."

His chin touching his chest, Owen's big eyes shone with unshed tears.

"And Oliver, what makes you think it's any business of yours whether or not Dillon's dad gets back together with his wife? For Dillon's sake, I hope they do remarry, but that's hardly for you to decide. As for him stealing me away from your father…" She shook her head. "That's ridiculous. I'm sorry about your dad leaving. You'll never know how much I ache inside for your pain, sweetie, but he's got a new family now, and he's not coming back. That doesn't mean he doesn't love you just as much. Just that he doesn't live here—and isn't going to live here—no matter how hard you wish he would."

"But why?" Oliver asked, making no attempt to hold back his tears. "I love him. Why doesn't he love me?"

"Oh, sweetie," she said, going to her son and kneeling, pulling him into a hug. "Your father adores you and Owen. He just has a funny way of showing it."

"I love you, too, Oliver." Owen hopped up from his chair to join the family hug. "I'm sorry I said all that stuff. I was just mad 'cause you called me a liar."

"I—I miss Dad," Oliver said. "I—I m-miss him so bad."

On her knees, rocking her two sobbing precious boys, Ella didn't miss Todd. She hated him. How could he have done this to their sons? Their family?

"M-Mom?" Oliver eventually said, his tears having subsided to the occasional hiccup.

"Uh-huh?" she asked, still holding him, still stroking his hair.

"Do I have to run away if Owen still lives here?"

finished they'd done their breakfast dishes and had moved on to play pool in the rec room. The space had been decorated by the captain's wife and looked more like a silk-flower factory explosion than an all-male workplace and hangout. The guys dreaded the day she got her hands on the rest of the place. Still, since she was the captain's wife, they'd all had to be polite and rave about how much they liked it. Blocking out the pink-and-blue floral wallpaper behind the pool table, Jackson finished his list of issues with the latest on Owen and Oliver's epic battle.

"Damn," the six-four Italian said, fingering his goatee while waiting for his turn, "you *have* gotten yourself into a mess. So on the one hand, the hot lady doctor is into you, and you're into her, but her kids can't stand you."

"Sad, but true."

"Then you've got your equally smokin' ex wanting to hook back up with you, but you're like, dude, been there, done that and ain't having it no more. But your kid is like, yes, Daddy, you *are* having it and then some." Spoken like a twenty-three-year-old. As the youngest in the station by ten years, sometimes translation was necessary to get the gist of what he was saying.

"Um, that's pretty much it—I think." Jackson was still trying to decipher portions of Calivaris's frat talk. "Got any advice?"

Calivaris took a second to ponder this. "Here's the deal. You gotta do what you gotta do."

Screwing up his face, Jackson asked, "Does that mean I've got to do what's right for my boy, or for me?"

"What feels good to you?" Calivaris was solids, and he hit his red into a corner pocket.

"That's the problem." Calivaris had missed his next shot, so Jackson tried getting his yellow stripe in the center pocket. "Sometimes, I'm on board with getting back with my ex. We used to have good times before she took off. And what about the pain she caused our son? How can I forget that?"

"Forget, hell. If you get back with her, you're going to have to totally forgive."

"And if I can't?"

"Easy," he said, making his next shot. "Go with another plan."

"Which would be?" Jackson asked, wincing when his pal sank yet another ball in the corner pocket.

"Get something going with the other woman whose twins hate you. Buy them lots of iPods and stuff. Trust me, they'll come around."

Jackson had to laugh. "How am I supposed to bribe kids with electronics on a fireman's salary?"

"Sorry, dude," he said, aiming for the eight ball, calling it, then sinking the shot. "I'm an idea man. If you're wanting construction documents, you'll have to find someone else."

"Got anyone in mind?" Jackson asked.

"My Grandma Vinnie's got a knack with tea leaves. Want me to give her a call?"

"Thanks, man," Jackson said, putting his cue back on the rack, "but I think I'll tackle this one on my own." Starting with calling the woman who occupied more and more of his thoughts.

Chapter Ten

"Hey," Jackson said to Ella early Saturday morning at the Key Elementary family yard sale. The school was raising money for new playground equipment. "I didn't know you were going to be here."

"The PTA wrangled me in to help." She looked especially pretty with her long hair in braids and a red school T-shirt nicely hugging her assets. Her khaki shorts gave a much better view of her legs than her usual slacks and lab coat. "Is Dillon here with you?"

He nodded. "And Julie. I wasn't planning on coming, but Dillon told her about the sale over dinner last night, and she thought it'd be good to clean out the closets, then do what we can to help."

"That was thoughtful of her." Instead of meeting his gaze, Ella glanced over her shoulder. "I'm sure once things get busy, we'll need the extra hands."

"You looking for someone? You seem distracted."

"No," she said, doing the same thing again. "I'm good. Owen and Oliver are around here somewhere with Rose. Dillon would probably enjoy hanging out with them." For a split second, a pained expression crossed her face, then she was off, heading toward a table piled with kids' clothes in need of folding.

Following, dodging a pigtailed second grader darting by clutching at least a dozen Barbies, he asked, "If I didn't know better, I'd say you were trying to avoid me."

"Why would I do that?" she said, not once looking his way.

"There you are," Julie said, holding Dillon's hand. With her free hand, she rubbed Jackson's back. Not too long ago, Ella had done the same, only her touch had sent sparks of awareness shooting down his spine. "Hi, Ella."

"Hi," Ella said, with what Jackson knew was her forced smile. "Nice seeing you again."

"Likewise." Julie turned her attention to Jackson. "Dillon and I found a sack filled with antique crystal doorknobs that'd look perfect in the house. Should I grab them?"

"Um, sure," he said, watching Ella fold faster. "That'd be great."

"We'll install them this afternoon. It'll be a fun family project, don't you think, Dillon?"

"Yep." Dillon grinned up at his mom, adoration etched into every inch of his face.

"Come on," Julie said to Jackson, tugging his hand, "I want you to see some antique stained-glass windows I found, too. They'd look great mounted at the top of the staircase. When the morning sun hits them just right, the whole entry hall will glow."

His imagination traveled back to Wednesday morning: Ella on her porch in her cute pink robe, her complexion glowing in the morning sun, those long legs of hers peeking out from between the parting in her robe.

He caught himself staring at Ella.

He forced a breath, knowing he should focus on Julie, but

having an awfully tough time of it. It irked him no end how the woman had forced her way back into his and Dillon's lives as abruptly as she'd left. It was as if it had never even occurred to her that Jackson might not want her back. Not that Dillon was giving him much of a choice.

"Jackson?" Julie elbowed his ribs. "What's the matter with you? You look like you have indigestion. Need an antacid?" To Ella, she said, "We just finished a huge country breakfast at Harriet's. You know, the cute new place out by the highway? Anyway, Jackson must've eaten his own weight in sausage gravy. I told him he'd pay for it later, and look, it hasn't even been an hour and already he's got a fire in his belly." When she took the liberty of rubbing his stomach, it was all Jackson could do not to push her away. Then he caught sight of his son grinning up at him.

"Mom's a good doctor, huh, Dad? She always knows just what to do to make us feel better."

"Thank you," Julie said, bending to give Dillon a kiss. "That's the nicest thing anyone's said to me all day."

Dillon preened.

Jackson fought down the sausage gravy that was indeed now making its way back up.

WOW…SHE THOUGHT, trailing after Owen and Oliver as they showed off her baby girl. She was gorgeous. Just as perfect as she remembered. Thank goodness she'd seen the ad about the school's yard sale in the newspaper.

Feeling especially bold in the morning sun, she gradually made her way over to the kids circled around a pile of toys for sale.

"Hi," she said, grabbing a model airplane. "Do any of you know how much this is?"

"It's a dollar, lady," a little boy told her, pointing to the tag on the plane's left wing. "See? It says so right there."

"Oh," she said with a laugh. "You're right. I'm sorry."

"That's okay," the boy said, returning to his play.

She browsed a few more minutes, all the while achingly aware of the closeness of her baby. She'd been dressed in another adorable outfit—this time, teeny baby jeans and a mini school T-shirt. A red baseball cap kept the sun from her precious eyes.

"That sure is a cute baby," she found the courage to say. "Is she your sister?" she asked Owen, who was hugging her close.

"Uh-huh," he said. "Wanna hold her?"

She took a moment to catch her breath and still her racing heart, then said, "Um, sure. That'd be nice."

As the boy gingerly passed off the infant to her, it was all she could do not to burst into happy tears. She clung to her child like a lifeline. If only she could wake each day holding her baby girl, everything would be okay. But how could she do that without her family being shamed?

Dragging in deep breaths of her baby's amazing scents of lotion and powder and everything good and sweet, she fought the aching knot in her throat.

I love you. I love you so much.

"Lady?" Owen asked, peering up at her. "Are you all right?"

"I—I'm great," she said, trying so very hard to mask the true intensity of her feelings. If she'd wanted, right now, she could take her baby and run. Run far away from the awful place that had forced her into this situation. No one should have to abandon their baby because they were afraid of what people might say or do.

"Lady? Are you crying?"

"N-no," she said, even though she was.

properly before slamming the side door and climbing behind the wheel.

"I'm ready," Oliver said, hopping in the front seat and fastening his seat belt. "I didn't think Holly Fleming was ever going to leave me alone."

The heat in the closed-up vehicle was stifling, and the second Ella started the engine, she turned on the air. Letting the lukewarm stream wash over her, she gripped the wheel with both hands, squeezing for all she was worth.

What had come over her? *Bite me?*

Inwardly groaning, she could only imagine the hell there'd be to pay for her one moment of speaking her mind. Marcia had had it coming, but still, for Ella to have gone off on her like that was so out of character. But then, speaking of character, the day had been incredibly trying, and Marcia's snide comments were the last straw.

Only to herself could Ella admit that yes, she very much cared for Jackson Tate. Probably more than she should in light of the fact that he and Julie were trying to patch things up, but that didn't lessen the way her stomach knotted with giddy tension every time he was around.

"I thought we were leaving," Oliver asked.

"We are," she said, putting the car in gear.

She was backing out of their parking place when, in her peripheral vision, she saw someone charging up behind the car. Braking, she glanced over her shoulder to find Jackson jogging up to the driver's-side window. Damn her stupid pulse for racing. He was just a friend, why couldn't her body seem to get that fact? She didn't want to hold him or kiss him or—

He knocked on the window.

She pressed the power button, sliding the window down. "Yes?"

"What's the hurry? You didn't even say goodbye."

Shrugging, she said, "It's been a long day. I'm ready to get home."

"I feel your pain," he said with the slow, sexy grin she'd grown so fond of. "I won't keep you, but Julie thought it might be nice if you and the boys and Rose came over for a barbecue tonight. I told her it might be—"

"No," Ella said, unable to fathom what spending a night with him and his wife might be like, especially since the last time she'd sat around the grill at his home had been so idyllic. "We have plans. Lots of plans."

"No, we don't, Mom." Oliver unfastened his seat belt, and crowded onto her lap. To Jackson, he asked, "Are you fixing more steaks?"

"If that's what you want," Jackson said.

"Yum, that sounds good." Owen bounded out of his seat, too. "Can we have a sleepover?"

"Sure." Jackson looked to Ella. "Assuming it's okay with your mom."

"They can go," she said, "but I'm busy. It's a work thing."

Talk to me, he said with his eyes. *It's me. Jackson. Your friend, remember?*

"Be sure and give my thanks to Julie for the invitation," she somehow managed. "It was nice of her to think of us."

"Ella…" His pause said everything. That he wanted to talk—*really* talk—but couldn't because of the boys.

"What time do you want me to drop off my guys?" she asked, looking anywhere but into his intense gaze.

"Whenever it's handy. For that matter, they can come with us now, if you'd like."

"Yeah!" the boys said in unison.

Cringing, Ella said, "I, ah, suppose that would be all right."

"Cool! Thanks, Mom!" Owen kissed her cheek.

"Yeah, thanks, Mom," Oliver said, gifting her with a fast hug.

"I'll be over," he said in a hushed tone when the boys were on the opposite side of the van. "I'm not sure when, but as soon as I can get away."

"Please, don't," she begged, not wanting to get involved deeper. They had nothing to discuss other than casual things such as whether he seriously wanted her to make her famous meatballs for his wedding reception. When he said nothing, just tortured her with his searching gaze, she repeated, "Please...."

With the tip of his finger, he traced her lips, whispering. "I'll see you tonight."

"WHERE ARE YOU OFF TO?" Julie asked while Jackson stood at the back door, SUV keys in hand. She'd been making Rice Krispies treats with the boys, and looked domestic wearing a pink apron she'd found tucked at the back of the pantry. She'd won it as a gag gift at one of her law office's Christmas parties. Everyone had thought it hilarious that their decidedly undomestic partner had won such a quintessentially Susie Homemaker gift.

"I've got to run a quick errand."

"What?" She was pressing the treats flat on the cookie sheet with the back of a wooden spoon.

"Just an errand. Does it matter?"

"You're lying. You're not running an errand. You're going to see Ella Garvey."

Expression grim, Jackson jiggled his keys. "What if I am?"

"Honey?" She fixed him with an accusatory stare, making him feel like a stranger in his own home. But then whenever she was here, he didn't feel as if he belonged. "I thought we were trying to work things out."

He sighed. "I just need to talk to her, all right? *Talk.*"

"You sure? Because at the school this afternoon, Marcia said—"

"Stop. Marcia Jenkins is a nasty gossip not even fit to say Ella's name. Now, if you're serious about wanting to patch things up with me, I'd suggest you lay off Ell. She's my friend. Nothing more." *Liar.* The deception caused bile to rose in his throat.

"I believe you," she said, giving him a quick hug and kiss. "Hurry back, though. I promised the boys we'd play Monopoly, and I don't want to start till you get home."

Home. Again, with Julie here, the place no longer felt like a home, but a mere house. Though Julie had designed the state-of-the-art kitchen with its black granite counters, stainless-steel appliances and custom cherry cabinets, she'd rarely—if ever—used any of it. His mother occupied the space more than his ex.

"Jackson?" Julie asked, cupping her hand to his cheek. "You okay?"

"Great," he said with a sharp laugh. "Never been better."

"I know this pouty tone." She sat on a stool at the counter bar. "Talk to me. What's on your mind?"

"You wanna know what's on my mind?" he asked, fingers gripping the back doorknob so tight, it hurt. "I'll tell you." He went to her, stopping inches from her face. "I don't get how all of a sudden, you've gone from wanting nothing to do with your family to spending every spare second with us. Volunteering at school yard sales? Baking? Playing Monopoly and going to craft fairs?" He snorted. "If I didn't know better, I'd say aliens have taken over the Julie I knew and used to love."

"I told you," she said, fisting his black golf shirt, tears pooling her eyes. "I've been lonely without you and Dillon, and then when he ran away, something inside of me snapped. I realized that somewhere along the line, my priorities had gotten screwed up. I'm sorry for that. You'll never know how sorry, but I can't change the past. All I can do is my best to right my wrongs." Tossing her arms around his neck, she fiercely hugged him. "I'm sorry. Please, at least try giving me a second chance. Don't you remember what we used to have?"

He had remembered. For two damned long years.

But he was tired.

"Say you love me," she asked, raining kisses on his cheeks and nose and lips. "Please, Jackson, say you still love me."

For their son's sake, with everything in him, Jackson wanted to grant her request. If he'd wanted to, he suspected he could've taken Julie upstairs and made love to her all night long. But a funny thing happened while she was kissing him. It wasn't her he fantasized about making love to, but Ella. Smart, funny, sweet, sweet Ella had somehow crept inside him and stolen his heart.

"The boys are outside," Julie said, voice raspy, "let's go upstairs to your room. *Our* room."

"I can't," he said, gently pushing her away, disentangling her arms from around his neck. "I just can't."

Eyes narrowed, still breathing heavy, Julie asked, "Is this about that errand you have to run?"

The hint of sarcasm behind her tone wasn't attractive. But then he supposed neither was the fact that he was going to see another woman when he'd just been kissing his past and possible future wife.

Chapter Eleven

"I thought you weren't coming," Ella said, Rose in her arms while she held the screen door half open. From somewhere inside, classical music played. Something sadly romantic with piano and strings. Night was falling fast, and she had no lights on in the house. Yet with the setting sun golden in her hair, she didn't need any.

"I told you I would, didn't I?"

"Yes, but—"

He stepped across the threshold, kissing her, kissing her. Losing himself in her taste, her spirit, the essence that was her. When he'd had his fill, he stepped back, pressing his thumb to her swollen lips. "I've wanted to do that all day."

"You shouldn't have," she said, circling his wrist, drawing his hand down, yet not letting go. "You shouldn't even be here."

"True," he said, but for once in his life not giving a flying damn about what he should and shouldn't do. "Got ice cream?"

Laughing, stepping aside to let him pass, she said, "Get in here, but fair warning, I'm out of peanut butter and chocolate chunk swirl."

"I consider myself warned."

"Okay, but first," she said, closing the door, then aiming

for the stairs, "I was just about to give the princess here her bath. Want to help?"

"Absolutely."

Ten minutes later, Jackson found himself on his knees in front of an old claw-foot tub. Inside the tub was another tub—a plastic mini one. Pink.

"Here," Ella said, passing Rose to him. "Hold her while I get the water ready."

With Rose thrust into Jackson's outstretched arms, Ella turned on the taps, adjusting the water, then tested it with the sensitive skin on her wrists. He vaguely remembered going through the same routine with Dillon, but they'd usually just bathed him in the kitchen sink. Julie had never been big on ceremony, and she'd plopped him in and out as efficiently as if she'd been rinsing a Thanksgiving turkey. He'd wanted to take pictures and savor the moments of Dillon's infancy, but she'd belittled him, calling him a sentimental sap.

"Got a strange question for you," he said, once Ella had taken the baby back and gotten her tub-ready.

"Shoot," she said, gingerly lying Rose in the water.

"Do you take lots of pictures of the twins?"

"Are you kidding me?" she asked, squirting a bead of yellow baby shampoo into a pink washing mitt. "Thank good-ness for the digital camera or I'd go broke developing film. We've already got hundreds of this cutie," she said, tickling the baby girl's sudsy tummy.

"Was that a grin?" he asked.

"Probably gas, but it sure looked like a tiny smile, didn't it?"

"Can't we just say it was?" Why, he couldn't have said, but it would mean a lot to him to witness one of Rose's firsts. With her, he found himself grasping a do-over mentality. He might not have gotten things perfect with Dillon, but with this one, he wanted to do things different. Better. He wanted to save this child the pain Dillon had been through. The only trouble was, Rose wasn't his. And Jackson for damned sure wasn't in any position to guarantee how her life might turn out.

"Sure," Ella said with a laugh so pretty it caused a hundred tiny fissures in his heart. "We can say whatever you want." One hand on the baby, she landed her other atop his head. Her fingers were warm and wet, rocking him with an erotic jolt.

"I think I'm falling in love with you…"

"W-what?" Her hand slowly fell, landing on his shirt collar, lingering warm water soaking through.

"You heard me. Got a towel?" he asked, nodding toward Rose. "Somebody's turning into a pink prune."

Expression dazed, she reached behind her to take a hooded pink towel from the bathroom counter. She handed it to him, and he, in turn, plucked Rose from the water and fumbled her into the makeshift robe. He cradled the infant, gingerly drying around her ears and under her arms and between impossibly small fingers and toes.

Jackson's admission had scared him. So much was riding on his reunion with Julie. His son's emotional well-being was at stake. He had no business telling any woman he loved her, but how could he help falling for Ella when she was everything he'd ever wanted all contained in one ultra-sexy package?

Carrying the infant to her nursery, ignoring the giant elephant in the room that had taken up occupancy alongside him, Jackson set Rose on her changing table. While Ella hovered behind him, worrying her lower lip, he lotioned the baby and diapered her. Dressed her in beruffled yellow pj's. By the time he got her kissed and hugged and settled in her crib, her eyes were already drifting shut.

"Goodnight, gorgeous," he whispered.

"I love you," Ella said, cupping her hand to Rose's head, yet looking at him.

His heart lurched. Was she talking to him, or the baby?

She left the room, gesturing for him to follow. After shutting Rose's nursery door, she leaned her shoulder against the wall, sighing and closing her eyes. "I—I love you, but I can't—*won't*—be anything beyond friends with you. It's not fair to Dillon."

"What about us, Ell? What's fair to you and me? Dammit," he said, taking her hands, easing his fingers between hers, "for the past few years, we've both been living a hell. Totally at the whim of our cheating spouses. When is it our turn to quit being the responsible ones, and do what *we* want?"

"When our kids head to college?" she asked with a strangled laugh, angling into him, slipping her arms around his waist and resting her cheek against his chest. "Face it, Jackson, like it or not, by default, Todd and Julie appointed us the grown-ups. We're our kids' last line of defense in teaching them right from wrong and values and morals. How's it going to look if I tell them what Todd did was wrong, but then turn around and do almost the same thing as him by having an affair with you?"

"Correct me if I'm wrong," he said, cupping her cheeks to tip her face back, granting him full access to her beautiful face, "but I'm not married. Neither are you. Yes, for Dillon, it would be great if I got back together with his mother, but what then? How long until the lie I'm living corrodes into ugliness? Fights and name-calling and eventually, another divorce? Only, this time, so contentious that Julie and I won't even be speaking? And since I'm now the bad guy in this scenario, what if she wins custody of my kid? And Dillon *is* mine, seeing how she abandoned him."

Sighing, Ella softly said, "You just proved my argument. There's too much at stake for us to explore whatever it is we're feeling. We hardly even know each other. Rose brought us together, but what happens when her mother's found? What do we have linking us when she's gone?"

This…he ached to say before kissing her till she was powerless to speak. Till she abandoned logic simply to feel. But he didn't kiss her. In fact, he released her hands so they weren't even touching. Could she be right? Was their affection for Rose, the urgency of the infant's situation, their only bond?

"What are you thinking?"

"I'm wondering if you're right," he admitted. "I'm wondering if my attraction to you is even real."

"Thanks," she muttered, turning her back on him to head down the stairs.

"I didn't mean I'm not turned on by you, Ell."

"Whatever," she said, continuing on to the kitchen where she yanked open the freezer and reached for the ice cream. She took a spoon from a drawer, then sat at the kitchen table, digging in.

"Do I get any of that?"

She shook her head. "Get your own. There's another half-dozen pints in the freezer."

"Stocking up in case of disaster?"

She coughed on her latest bite. "Where you're concerned, Jackson Tate, every day's become a disaster."

"YOU TOLD HIM you love him?" Rachel asked Monday during a rushed deli lunch. Shock raised her eyebrows a good inch. "Have I taught you nothing?"

"Relax," Ella said, biting into her ham and Swiss. "He said it first."

"Like that makes it better?" Ella's friend returned her roast beef and cheddar to a chip-filled basket. "I need details in order to adequately interpret this sudden turn of events."

"What you need," Ella said, rolling her eyes, "is a chill pill. It's no biggie—and I saw that."

"What?" Rachel asked, pretending she hadn't just deeply inhaled the secondhand smoke wafting over from the deli's miniscule smoking section.

"You know what. I'm proud of you for hanging in there so long. Keep up the good work."

"Nice try at changing the subject," Rachel complained, digging in her purse for her gum, "but get back to those details."

Shrugging, Ella said, "We both confessed our undying love, but as rational, reasonable adults, we came to the conclusion that it wouldn't work out between us."

"Meaning—" Rachel chomped hard on a pickle "—the all-sainted twins wouldn't approve?"

"Hey!" Her friend's latest comment struck a nerve for Ella. Suddenly, the movie-poster-filled walls of Five Star Deli closed in on her. The sounds of the Star Wars soundtrack and the beeping cash register and chattering diners were too much. "Those are my kids you're talking about. I don't live in a vacuum. What they think matters."

"Know what else matters?" Not waiting for a reply, Rachel forged ahead with, "Your happiness. Do you think those kiddos of yours are going to be content if you're moping all the time? Or subsisting solely on peanut butter and chocolate chunk swirl?"

"I added a new flavor—mint fudge ripple."

Rachel shook her head.

"Another thing that occurred to me is the whole Rose issue. What if Jackson doesn't really love me, but the idea of me?

You know, the whole cute baby thing? But one of these days, Hank's going to track down Rose's mom, and then Jackson's going to dump me like a—"

"Stop." Holding out her hands, Rachel said, "If I have to hear one more lame reason for why Jackson doesn't really love you, I'm going to hurl. Have you ever considered the reasons why he would love you—regardless of whether you have Rose?"

"No."

"Of course, not. So right now, let's list them, shall we?" Taking out her checkbook, Rachel ripped off a deposit slip, then wrote as she spoke. "Number one, you're gorgeous."

"Try thirty pounds overweight."

"You're gorgeous," Rachel repeated, ignoring Ella's objections. "You're a complete brainiac—although I suppose some guys might find that a turn-off. Luckily, Jackson seems pretty secure in his own skin, meaning he doesn't view your success as a threat."

"Shouldn't we head back to the clinic?" Ella asked, tapping her watch.

"Shouldn't you hush it? Now, where was I? Oh—three, funny. Four, sweet. Five, compassionate. Six—"

"Rachel, while I appreciate the sentiment behind this, we need to get going."

"True," her friend said, wadding her napkin and tossing it into the basket, "but I want you to have this." She handed Ella the list she'd headed: Ella's Lovable Traits. "Tape it to your bathroom mirror and review it every morning when you wake and every night before going to bed."

"Yes, ma'am," Ella teased, giving her friend a mock salute before dumping her sandwich remains in the trash.

"Honey, I'm serious," Rachel said, hand on her arm. "More

than anyone I know, you deserve to be happy. Kids bounce back. They adjust. Yes, in the short run, you and Jackson taking things public might be rocky, but in the long run, I think you two make a solid pair."

On the short walk to the office, warm sun giving her a much-needed hug, Ella secretly agreed with her friend. Jackson seemed better for her than Todd ever had. Unfortunately, that didn't change the fact that for all practical purposes, he was taken. When push came to shove, he'd return to his family. That was just the kind of honorable man Jackson Tate was. Which only made Ella pine for him more.

IT WAS TUESDAY NIGHT when Jackson saw Ella again. She was at the hospital emergency room, consulting on a five-year-old female burn victim he'd carried from her flame-filled bedroom. The girl had been playing with Mommy's lighter and set a pile of stuffed animals on fire. She had burns over sixty percent of her body and was on the verge of being Life-Flighted to a Kansas City burn-specialty ICU.

It wasn't in Jackson's job description to accompany the ambulance to the hospital, but something about the hollow look in the girl's eyes had driven him here. He had to know she'd be all right.

"Hey, man," Calivaris said, patting his back, "the girl's going to live. You did all you could."

"I know," Jackson said, studying the intensity on Ella's face as she stabilized the girl for travel. He found it ironic that Julie's job as a criminal attorney was saving scumbags from having to go to prison, whereas he and Ella were in essentially the same business of looking after people's health and well-being. Maybe that's why he was so attracted to her—because they spent their time trying to make the world a better place?

Within thirty minutes, Ella had briefed the flight team on the girl's vitals, then they were off.

Jackson supposed he should head back to the station, but Calivaris was off chatting up a buxom brunette admittance clerk, and from where he sat alongside a half-dead potted palm in a quiet corner of the E.R. waiting room, the view was just too good. Ella in her sexy lab coat, completing paperwork. Ella comforting family. Ella helping a nurse set a teen's broken arm. She didn't have a clue he was there, which, in light of their last meeting, was probably a good thing.

Why had he told her he loved her? Why hadn't he just kept the fact to himself? After all, it wasn't as if he could do anything about it. She'd called him a disaster—well, not him per se, but her emotional state whenever she was around him. That couldn't be a good sign.

She glanced his way.

Had she felt his stare?

She waved.

He waved.

"Ready?" Calivaris stopped in front of him.

"I guess," Jackson said, dodging to try and see Ella around his friend's hulking frame.

"I've got a date. See that chick over there?" He gave a finger wave to the brunette he'd been with. "We're having drinks when she gets off. She's hot, huh?"

"Sure." Dammit. Where had Ella gone? One minute, she'd been there, and now she'd—

"Hi, Jackson," she said, popping out from behind Calivaris. "I heard you were the one who pulled Mandy from her room."

"Wish I'd've got there sooner."

"With grafting, she'll be all right. In the next few weeks, though, she's in for a lot of pain."

Jackson introduced her to his friend, who said a polite goodbye, and then was back to his brunette, telling Jackson to give a holler when he was ready to go.

"He seems nice," Ella said, looking politely distracted.

"Yeah. Calivaris is a great guy." Was he imagining it, or was there an awkward vibe between them that had never been there before? "Who's with Rose and the twins?"

"My friend Claire, from down the street. If Hank doesn't make progress soon in finding Rose's birth mother, I'm going to recommend Claire and her husband be considered for Rose's possible adoptive parents."

"You must really like these people," he said, scuffing the tiled floor with the tip of his right shoe.

"I do. They've tried for years to have a baby. Rose would be an incredible blessing to them."

"More than she has been to you?"

Her stricken expression hit him like a blow. "What's that supposed to mean? Are you implying I don't care about Rose?"

"No. Hell, no. All I meant was that—"

"I've got to go," she said, already turning away.

"Ella…" On his feet, he snagged her lab coat's sleeve. "What's wrong with you? Why are you—"

"Not here," she practically hissed. "I seriously don't want to get into this here."

"Get into what?" he asked in an urgent whisper. "I didn't even know there was anything wrong."

"Are you kidding me?" Glancing over her shoulder, then back to him, she said, "I thought we'd said everything there was to say Saturday night, but the more I think about it, the madder I get." Her sharp tone had attracted the attention of a snoopy, gossipy type craning her neck to get a better view. "Come here," Ella said, leading him to a supply closet filled with antiseptic-smelling cleaning supplies and a fresh-linen cart.

"Are we allowed to be in here?" he asked.

"Don't be a dork." She flicked on the overhead lights.

"What? I'm just asking."

She sighed, closing the door behind her. "Back to our previous conversation, how dare you tell me you love me, when you've got Julie and your son under the impression that everything's hunky-dory with them?"

"Hunky-dory?" He raised his eyebrows.

"I'm serious," she said. "I told you I won't be a party to—"

"You look gorgeous when you're mad. Your eyes all sparking and nostrils flared."

"Mmm...that does sound attractive. Back to the topic at hand, you've got to—"

"Marry me," he said. "Forget all the reasons we shouldn't be together and go with your heart. You know Dillon loves you and your boys have always liked me. Together, we'll be an amazing family. We can adopt Rose. She'll be our team mascot."

"A-are you kidding me?" she asked with a strangled cough. "The whole notion is ludicrous. You're getting back together with Julie. We haven't even been on a date."

Pressing her against the wall, he kissed her hard. Like there was no tomorrow. Maybe because for them, there might not be. Yes, considering they hadn't even been on an official date, the topic of marriage was nuts. But then so was the thought of getting back together with a woman like Julie, who'd stomped on his heart.

"Y-you've got to stop doing that," she said right before kissing him back, easing her fingers into his hair with a decidedly feminine moan.

"I will," he promised. "Right after this..." Feeling like a

teen making out under the high-school bleachers, he lived for the moment, losing himself in Ella's minty flavor and faint floral smell.

Breathing hard, foreheads touching, she said, "It's the craziest thing, but I *want* to marry you. With every part of my being, I want to share raising my boys with you and cook dinners with you and wash cars and go to PTA and—"

"Whoa," he said, with a faint grin, "I draw the line at PTA."

"I don't blame you. But Jackson, as beautiful as this dream is, it will never work. Dillon would end up resenting us both."

"Stop," he said, easing his hand under her lab coat, smoothing it along the soft, warm small of her back. "No one said we had to run into this. We'll take our time. The kids will get used to us."

"Do you really want that?" she asked, palms flattened against his chest. "Waiting for our children to get *used* to having a stepmom or dad? Wouldn't you rather be in a relationship you can publicly celebrate?"

"So then your answer to my proposal is no?"

"Jackson…" She groaned. "You know you didn't really mean it. It was a spur-of-the-moment impulse you should've held in check."

She was right about the spur-of-the-moment thing, but he didn't regret having said it. He didn't even understand why he'd asked, but now that he had, he was at peace about it. He certainly wouldn't be withdrawing the question. "There's something about you, Ell, I can't resist. I want to be with you—your boys and Rose. I don't want to be lonely anymore."

"Unfortunately," she said, eyes shiny, "the ramifications of keeping company with me may end up making you more lonely than ever."

Chapter Twelve

"He what?" In Exam Room Three, Rachel covered her gum-crammed mouth with her hands while shrieking. "No way. The man *did not* ask you to marry him. What did you say?"

"What do you think I said? No. Absolutely, not." But she'd wanted to marry him on the spot. She'd wanted to slip into a comfortable new life the way she might escape a rotten day by tugging on her favorite jammies. Jackson soothed her. Made her feel better the way nothing ever had, save her most beloved flavors of ice cream.

"Hmmm…" Rachel perched on the end of the exam table, crinkling the white sanitary paper. "I never saw this coming."

"Like I did?" Dropping to sit on a padded rolling stool, Ella sighed. "We've never even been out to dinner, yet I feel I've always known him. You should see how gentle he is with Rose. And with the boys, he's fun-loving, yet firm. After he had to rescue them from the pizza place's hamster tubes, he sat them all down for the cutest lecture. Telling them not to panic in tight spots and to think their way through difficult times. Oliver drank it all in. He craves Todd's attention, and while Jackson can't replace Owen and Oliver's father, I really think that—"

"Would you listen to yourself?" Rachel said. "You've practically talked yourself in to running off to elope."

Hands to her flaming cheeks, Ella said, "You're right. What am I going to do?"

"I think the better question is, what do you *want* to do?"

"Oh, no," Ella said, actually trembling from the force of her emotions. "That's not fair, because if I could just do what I wanted, there wouldn't even be an issue. There are so many lives at stake it makes my head spin. The logical side of me knows even to think of such a thing as marrying a practical stranger is ludicrous, but knowing Dillon as I do has made me feel as if I've been intimately acquainted with his father for equally long."

Rachel blew a bubble. "You've got it bad, girl."

"Tell me about it."

Paige poked her head through the door. "Sorry to bug you, doc, but your next patient's ready."

"Thanks," Ella said with a sigh.

Rachel hopped off the exam table to give her a hug. "You'll figure this out."

"I know," she said with a faint smile. "The only question is when?"

"This is a nice surprise," Ella said that night, holding the door open for her friend Claire. "What's up?"

"You tell me," Claire said with a suggestive wink, pushing her way in.

"Miss Claire!" Owen said, jumping up from in front of the living-room TV to hug the petite blonde. "Are you going to babysit us?"

"Yep," she said, giving him an affectionate kiss atop his head. "And look what I brought." She wagged what looked like an old-school video game.

"Cool! I'm gonna go get Oliver, then we can play."

"Okay," Ella said, hands on her hips. "Mind telling me what this is all about?"

"I could, but that would leave you with less than five minutes to get ready for your big date."

"I don't have a date."

"Oh, yes you do…."

By the time Jackson arrived, Ella was a bundle of nerves. Beyond the usual issues of what to wear and what to do with her hair, she was scared the boys were going to put two and two together to come up with four. They were highly observant. They knew Mom didn't usually get dressed up at seven, then leave the house with a man.

When the doorbell rang, she was checking herself out in the mirror, wishing her favorite pale-yellow sundress didn't cling to her hips and breasts. She really needed to lay off the ice cream. And she would. Just as soon as she figured out what to do about Jackson.

Forcing a deep breath, Ella smiled at her reflection, telling herself she could get through the evening without being attracted to the guy. She could stop her cravings to kiss him and wouldn't touch him even once. Well… Maybe just once—but that was seriously it!

From the top of the stairs she heard the muffled sounds of Jackson coaching the boys on whatever game Claire had brought.

"This is awesome!" Oliver shouted. "Look how many mushrooms I've already got."

"Don't get too cocky," Jackson warned. "This level is notorious for—"

"Aw, man. He fell off the cliff."

"Told you," Jackson said. "Next time, watch your speed around that curve and you'll do fine."

Pausing at the foot of the stairs, Ella closed her eyes and clutched her stomach. Butterflies had turned into darting, gigantic moths.

She jolted when strong, warm hands eased around her waist, then a masculine voice whispered in her ear, "Relax. You look amazing."

"My dress is too tight," she blurted. "I have to stop eating, and—"

"Your dress—and, more specifically, your sexy curves—are taking my breath away. And if you stopped eating, who be would my late-night ice cream buddy?"

Ella's throat tightened and tears sprang to her eyes. How did Jackson always know the perfect thing to say?

"Ready?"

She nodded. To Claire, she said, "Thank you."

"No problem. You guys have fun."

"Mom?" Owen asked.

"Yes, hon?"

"Wherever you're going, can you bring back French fries?"

"We're not going to that kind of place," Jackson said.

"Where are you going?" Owen wanted to know.

"It's a surprise."

"Will there be snow?" Owen's eyes got big.

"You're stupid," Oliver said, slugging his shoulder.

"Ouch! What'd you do that for?"

"Boys!" Ella interjected before things got too out of hand. "Behave for Miss Claire."

"Yes, Mommy." Owen leaped up to give her a hug. Oliver was right, she thought with an inner grin. His little brother was a suck-up.

"Are you going on a date?" Oliver asked, pausing in his game to stare down Jackson.

"You could call it that," Jackson said. "Is that all right? Maybe I should have asked you first, seeing how you're the oldest and that makes you man of the house."

Warmth flowed through Ella. Again, Jackson had known the right thing to say.

"I guess you can go," Oliver said, raising his chin. "But I don't like it."

"I appreciate your honesty," Jackson said. "That's an admirable quality for a man."

Still staring, Oliver shoved his hands in his shorts pockets. "Thanks."

To Ella, Jackson said, "Ready?"

She nodded, then gave both boys a hug. "I love you."

"Love you, too, Mommy." Owen kept right on hugging her while Oliver glared.

"I've got to go," Ella said, prying Owen's arms from her waist. "Be back soon."

At Jackson's SUV, he held the passenger-side door open for her, helping her in. Once he climbed inside, his nearness consumed her. She wanted to run her fingers through the back of his short, spiky hair. Skim her fingertips along the powerful ridges of his shoulders and chest.

"You okay with this?" he asked, slipping the key into the ignition. "I know it's short notice, but I work tomorrow, and this was a perfect night for my folks to take Dillon, and then Julie will be back in town, so—"

"I'm wonderful with this," she admitted, resting her head against the seat back while he reversed out of the narrow drive. "But I shouldn't be."

"If it makes you feel better, this weekend I'm telling Julie

I'd welcome her being more involved in our son's life, but that I don't see wedding bells in our future."

"But—"

He silenced her with the softest of kisses before backing out onto the quiet neighborhood street. "Can you just once enjoy yourself in the moment without constantly trying to keep abreast of oncoming disaster?"

"I'll try," she said, covering his hand on the gearshift. "But it's kind of hard when you head out on your first date in years only to be glared down by your son."

"He'll get over it." Jackson turned the vehicle left, then made a quick right.

"Where are we going?"

"It's a surprise."

"Oh." The way her life had been going as of late, she wasn't sure she still liked surprises.

"Promise," he said, squeezing her hand. "This one's good."

After a few more minutes, seeing how he needed two hands on the wheel for their latest turn—off the road and into a field—Jackson released her. She'd barely had time to ponder already missing his touch when the SUV bucked and rocked in protest of the transition from smooth blacktop to knee-high weeds and grasses.

"I hate to be a party pooper," she said, teeth rattling from the rough ride, "but I would have been perfectly happy with a quiet steak supper."

"Nah," he said, casting a wicked sexy grin her way, "too boring."

They'd crossed the sunset-washed field to enter forest slanted with hazy rays. The ride had considerably smoothened when Jackson joined up with a four-wheel drive path. It was deeply rutted, but as long as the SUV's tires straddled them, at least her teeth didn't feel in danger of being knocked from her head.

"Okay," she asked, "you've got me curious. Where are we?"

"Patience, my dear."

Laughing, she said, "Sorry, but that has never been one of my strong suits."

"Then it's a good thing you're getting practice."

She stuck out her tongue.

A few minutes later, in shadowy twilight, the vehicle's headlights shone upon the ghostly paddlewheeler. It seemed as if a lifetime had passed since they'd last seen it. In full sunlight, it had been derelict and sad. In the purples and oranges of the last of the day, vines embraced the behemoth, flowing and undulating like the water the craft should have been in.

"It's gorgeous," she said, throat knotted with still-fresh emotions from their tumultuous last visit here. "What made you think of coming to this place?"

"I felt as if we had unfinished business here," he said, turning off the engine. "I acted like a buffoon, and seeing how I've always been fond of this old boat, I wanted to rechristen it with happy memories instead of sad."

"But we learned our boys were safe here," she pointed out.

"But because of my confusion over Julie, I also went off on you here. And for that, I'm sorry."

"It's okay," she said, removing her seat belt so she could better face him.

"Ready?" he asked.

"For what?"

"Your big surprise. Come on," he said, opening his door. "Let's go."

She followed him into a clearing where he'd set up camp chairs and made a rock-ringed fire pit into which logs had already been laid. On a nearby blanket were two coolers and neatly stacked plates, napkins and forks, spoons and knives, a cast-iron skillet and aluminum foil. The nicest item was a wildflower bouquet around which he'd tied an awkward yellow bow.

"Jackson…" she said, tearing up at his thoughtfulness.

"I made your bow yellow, because you seem to like that color."

"I love that color," she said, tossing her arms around him for a hug. "Thank you."

"So you like it?"

"Are you kidding?" she asked. "I love it. I haven't been on a picnic in forever. What're we having to eat?"

"As soon as I get a fire going, we'll have those steaks you were craving, baked potatoes and asparagus."

"I'm impressed," she said. "But how are you going to fix all of that on a camp fire?"

"Trust me," he said with a manly thump to his chest. "I've got skills."

"THIS IS SERIOUSLY embarrassing," Jackson said twenty minutes later beneath the last gasp of fading sun. "How could I have remembered to haul all of this crap out here, and yet forgotten a lighter or matches?"

"It happens," she said with an annoying, albeit adorable, giggle.

"This isn't funny, Ell. I've been planning this for a couple of days. I wanted to show you a nice time away from the boys. You know, remind you you're a woman and I'm a man, and though it may not seem like it at times, there is more to our lives than kids."

"No way," she teased. "You're making that up."

"Woman…" he warned, snagging her around her waist with a playful growl. "I'm already grumpy enough about our lack of fire. Don't make things worse."

"What if I did this?" she asked, torturing him with a trail of kisses around the base of his neck.

"Then you'd really be in trouble," he said, instantly aroused, instantly craving far more than the slabs of pricey meat languishing in the cooler. "Not that I'm complaining, but—"

"Hush," she said, silencing him with her lips. Oh, but the woman had a way with kisses.

Coming up for air, he said, "Not that I haven't thoroughly enjoyed your appetizers, but I'm starving. What do you want to do about dinner?"

"Did you bring anything for dessert? We could just pig out on that."

"Um, yeah," he said with a grim set to his lips. "I, ah, sort of figured on heading back to your place for ice cream."

Grinning, shaking her head, she said, "How about we switch to plan B?"

"Which is?" He smacked a whiny mosquito about to land on his forearm.

"We pack all of this up, head back to town, rent a movie then take all the food to your grill."

"What about your ice cream?"

"Simple," she said, swatting a swarm of pesky gnats. "We rent the movie from the grocery store, then pick up a few cartons of what we will from henceforth call *your* ice cream."

SAVE FOR THE UNEASY ball of doubt in her stomach—the one she was actively choosing to ignore—Ella couldn't remember having ever been more content. She and Jackson had made a delicious meal, eaten it by candlelight in his quiet kitchen, and they now shared a chaise lounge on his patio, looking up at the stars.

"Thanks again," she said, "for the picnic. It was an incredibly thoughtful gesture."

"Even without food?" he asked, kissing her left eyebrow.

"Especially without food. It proved you're human and not just the hunky paragon of perfection I had you pegged for."

Leaning into her, kissing her cheeks and the tip of her nose, he said, "Mom always told me to beware of wenches with forked tongues."

"You didn't seem to mind this tongue of mine a few minutes ago."

"You got me," he said, feigning chest pains.

When they'd both stopped laughing, as much as Ella hated breaking the languid mood, there were things needing to be said. "Jackson..."

"Oh no, here it comes..."

"What are you talking about?" she asked, pulling back to better see his face. He was so handsome in the flickering glow of the citronella candles. Strong brow, high cheekbones covered in a hint of stubble. Eyes so deep and rich she could lose herself in them. Looking at him sometimes hurt, as though he was a dream that would fade with morning sun.

"Judging by the pained expression on your gorgeous face, this is the part of the evening when you tell me you had a great time, but can't see me again."

She sighed.

"I'm right?"

"No. Not entirely, anyway."

He groaned.

"Hear me out." Toying with the buttons of his shirt, she searched for the right words. "The other night, you asked me a question, and at the time, as amazing as the prospect of spending the rest of my life with you sounded, I didn't take you seriously. But after thinking about it—while I'm not saying I think we should jump into anything—I do believe your idea to have merit, and as such—"

"Wait a minute," he said, sitting up on the oversized chaise, "are you presenting an oral dissertation or giving me an affirmative answer on my marriage proposal?"

Pulse pounding in her ears, she licked her lips. "What I think I'm saying is that I love you. I don't know how or when it happened, or why or—" she lowered her gaze "—or if I even wanted it to happen. But if you're serious about ending things with Julie, I—I'd really like to explore—"

He pulled her into a kiss that nearly made her weep with joy. Never had her heart been more full. Yet in the same breath it occurred to her how much sorrow this decision would bring Jackson's son.

"You've made me so happy," he said. "We're going to make a great life together. You, me, Rose and our guys."

"I agree," she said, trailing her fingers over his dear face, exploring every inch. "Together, we're going to make a great team, but telling the boys will be tough. What are you going to say to Dillon?"

"The truth…" He blew out a breath. "At first, he's not going to be happy, but that shouldn't make you feel bad. I'll have a good talk with him. Make him understand."

"Still…" Stomach tight with nerves, she said, "I don't want him to hate me. I couldn't stand it if he were to think of me as the woman who drove away his mom."

"Trust me," he assured with the sweetest, softest of kisses. "Everything's going to turn out fine. We won't rush into this, but take it nice and slow. Give everyone time to adjust. Including us." Kissing him again, Ella tried abandoning herself to pure feeling. She tried forgetting the tough times she and Jackson surely had ahead. But trying and actually succeeding were two vastly different things. Jackson made it all sound easy. Tell Julie, tell the boys—maybe even keep Rose. But if there was one thing Ella had learned in her lifetime, it was that nothing worth having came easily. Her medical career hadn't, bringing her twins into the world hadn't, and the hot and cold sensations suddenly seizing her system told her that marrying Jackson Tate one day might be her toughest challenge of all.

Chapter Thirteen

"Nice shirt," Oliver said, pointing to Dillon's Transformers T-shirt. Owen was on his other side. They sat in the third row of Mindy's mom's minivan. Luckily for them, the girls were in the row ahead of them.

"Thanks," Dillon said. "Last time she was here, my mom brought it for me from Kansas City. She said she thought it would make me look older."

"Oliver?" Mrs. Ford called from her seat behind the steering wheel. "Is your seat belt fastened?"

"Yes, ma'am," he said, clicking it around him really fast before she could see.

"Thank you."

"Where were you last night?" Oliver asked his friend.

"My grandma and grandpa's. We had fish for dinner. It was gross."

"Sorry," Oliver said, digging for gum in his backpack.

"It's okay."

Because his friend was bummed about having to eat fish, Oliver wasn't sure if this was the right time to mention the awful news he had, but he didn't want Dillon to get all mad at school, so he figured now was probably the best time.

Clearing his throat the way he'd heard his dad do just before telling him bad stuff, Oliver said, "Dillon, something pretty awful happened last night."

"What?"

Owen stopped putting basketball stickers in Mindy's hair. "You're not going to tell him about Mom and his dad's date, are you? 'Cause if you do, he's gonna get real mad."

"What!" Dillon made fists and growled.

"Told you," Owen said.

"*Eeeuuw!*" Mindy complained, feeling the back of her head. "What did you put in my hair?"

"Doesn't your mom know my dad's marrying my mom?" Dillon asked.

Oliver shrugged.

"Maybe they had a really bad time?" Owen suggested.

"Yeah, I'll bet so," Dillon said. "'Cause I know my dad wouldn't like anyone but my mom."

"What if he does?" Oliver asked.

"I'll hate him forever."

"Yeah," Owen said. "Me, too."

Mindy said, "I hate all of you."

"Julie," Jackson said, glancing up from the newspaper he'd been reading at the kitchen table to see his ex-wife silhouetted in the door frame. He'd just gotten Dillon off to school, and was enjoying a second cup of coffee. "You're early."

"Yep." Removing a light jacket, she folded it over the back of one of the table's six chairs. He hadn't been expecting her till six or seven that night. "I wasn't feeling well, so I took the day off."

"Nothing serious, I hope?"

"Just a cold."

"Want me to make you some tea?" he asked, already standing.

"Yes, please."

"Toast? Cereal?" He found the kettle in a cabinet beneath the stove.

"No, thank you."

"If you weren't feeling well, Julie, you should've called. Dillon would understand if you couldn't make it." Filling the kettle with water, he put it on the stove, lighting the gas burner.

"I know. But the moment you told me he was missing, I promised God—myself—I would never again hurt or disappoint our little boy. Sick or healthy, there's nowhere I'd rather be than here."

"Fair enough." She looked tired. Her usual flawless makeup was absent, and now that he'd had a moment to study her, in place of her usual dark-toned business attire she wore a gray jogging suit and sneakers. Her normally sleek hair was pulled back into a loose ponytail that made her look more like the woman he'd married.

The kettle whistled, and Jackson took it off the burner, then rummaged through cabinets for tea and a mug. "Sugar?"

"Sweetener, if you have it."

"Nope."

"Sugar's fine, then. Thanks."

Was it just him, or had they become strangers? He'd had more meaningful conversations over having his groceries scanned and sacked.

He'd set her steaming mug to the table when she rose, appeared disoriented, then collapsed as if someone had pulled her plug.

"Julie!" he cried. "Honey, wake up."

In an instant, she was back, but her color was off.

Scooping her into his arms, he carried her to the living-room sofa, settling her gently on the cushions, propping throw pillows beneath her head.

"Wh-what happened?" she asked, voice scratchy and weak.

"You fainted," he said. "Is something else going on with you—other than this cold?"

"Not that I know of," she said, hand to her forehead.

"When was the last time you ate?" His innate concern for her caught him off guard. The moment she'd crumpled at his feet, she'd unwittingly shown him a vulnerable side she'd always pretended didn't exist. They'd once argued about the fact that no matter what—even when her father had died— she'd maintained a tough exterior. Never had she let anyone inside—even him.

"I don't know. Maybe sometime yesterday. I was in court late, then had to go back to the office to talk strategy with a new client."

"Stay put," he said, smoothing stray hairs from her forehead. "I'll fix you scrambled eggs and toast."

Smiling up at him, eyes drowsy, she nodded. "Thank you. Sorry to be a bother."

"It's no trouble," he said, hustling to the kitchen. "Be right back."

He'd nearly finished Julie's meal when the phone rang. So deep was he in thought that the ringing made him flinch as he turned off the stove. He burned his pinky and brought it to his mouth.

"Hello?" he answered, not even looking at the caller ID.

"Hey, handsome. How are you?" In the split second it'd taken to recognize Ella's voice, his emotions went from gratitude at hearing her voice, to the realization that if he were any sort of gentleman he'd have to put off telling Julie of his plan to pursue a relationship with Ella, at least until she felt better.

"I'm all right," he said, "but Julie's here and she just fainted."

"Want me to come over?"

He was touched by the offer, but refused. "She said she has a cold and hasn't eaten in a while, so I made eggs. If that doesn't perk her up, I'll give you a call."

"Why did she even come if she feels so bad?"

"I asked the same thing," he said, again putting his burned pinky to his mouth to ease the sting. "She said she didn't want to disappoint Dillon by not coming."

"Oh. That's nice." Did he detect a note of sarcasm in her tone.

"What's the matter?" he asked with a chuckle. "Afraid she might give you a run for your money in the sainthood department?"

A long pause told him his joke hadn't been well received. "Do you honestly think I'm so petty as to consider myself a saint, and think poorly of another mother who wants to be with her son?"

"Aw, come on, Ell," he urged. "Lighten up. I was only teasing."

"Well, in light of the fact that a few days ago you were still considering marrying the woman, I don't think you're funny. I still have serious reservations about our dating. The ramifications for Dillon are—"

"Ell," he said as sternly as possible without coming across as a brute. "I promise, it was a joke, albeit, a bad one. Remember Marcia Jenkins? Face it, if we do end up together, you'll have to work on teaching me a true sense of humor."

"*If? If* we end up together?" she asked, voice uncharacteristically small.

"Sweetheart, come on. You're overanalyzing every little thing I say. I love you, all right? I fully plan on telling Julie the truth of my feelings just as soon as she feels human again."

"Jackson!" Julie shouted from the living room. "Is everything okay?"

"Fine!" he hollered back, covering the phone's mouthpiece. "Be right there." To Ella, he said, "Gotta go. I'll call later, though, okay?"

"Sure. Tell Julie I hope she feels better."

"DR. GARVEY?"

"Yes," Ella said, standing at the front door, a fitful Rose in her arms. The weather was atrocious and perfectly suited to Ella's dour mood. Rain fell in undulating sheets, and the middle-aged woman on the porch was soaked, despite carrying an umbrella and wearing a red rain slicker.

"I'm so sorry to drop in on you, but the school principal seemed to think it was urgent I contact you as soon as possible." Flashing a faint smile, she said, "I'm Ruth Busby, a cafeteria worker at the school your sons attend. Key Elementary?"

"Yes. Please, won't you come in?" Ella stepped back, allowing the dripping woman to pass. Rose's whining escalated into a full-blown wail. "May I take your coat?"

"Oh, no," Ruth said. "You've got your hands full, so I'll only stay a minute. I would've called, but my cell's not getting any reception in this weather, and since I've seen the boys playing out front on sunny days, and it's on my way home, I figured it'd be just as easy to stop by."

Rose continued to wail. "Sorry," Ella said with an apologetic wince. "It's past feeding time, and we just got home."

"I'll make this extra brief, then. Today at lunch, I was washing down tables when I overheard your little Owen telling a friend about the 'crying lady' at the school yard sale. He said he'd been afraid she was going to steal Rose from him, and he had to beg her to give Rose back. Now, mind you, I'm not ordinarily in the business of eavesdropping on the students, but seeing how pretty much everyone in town knows about your mystery baby, I thought this might be an important clue to help the sheriff find her mother."

"Thank you," Ella said, stunned and disappointed Owen had said nothing to her. "I'll be sure to ask my son to relay all he knows about this mystery woman to the sheriff."

Ruth nodded, wished her a good evening, then was off into the rapidly falling night.

Closing the door, Ella shouted above Rose's ear-splitting wails, "Owen Eli Garvey! Get your booty down here!"

"FEELING BETTER?" Jackson asked Julie, delivering his mother's homemade chicken noodle soup and crackers to the guest bedroom. She sat up in the bed, a half-dozen pillows behind her. Dillon cuddled alongside her, contentedly looking at a photo album of a long-ago trip to Miami.

"A little," she said.

Outside, for an instant, lightning turned dark to light. Thunder rolled.

"This is some storm we're having, huh?" He set the tray on her bedside table.

Nodding, she said, "Hope the power doesn't go out. Remember that Thanksgiving when we had all your crazy cousins down from Idaho and we lost power?"

Smiling at the reminiscence of his grumbling, hungry cousins staring in disbelief at the raw turkey, he said, "How could I forget the incident that prompted us to switch over to all gas appliances?"

Sharing in their laughter, Dillon asked, "Is that the year Grandma June took us all out for Chinese food?"

"You remember?" Julie asked.

"Uh-huh," he said, after covering a big yawn. "I got a *really* good fortune cookie. It said I'm going to be rich."

"Excellent," Jackson said, sitting on the foot of the bed. "Does that mean from now on, you'll be paying for the house and car?"

"No way!" their son exclaimed. "I'm buying nothing but gum and video games."

"Nice," Jackson said with a nod. "I'll try the same with my next check."

"You?" Julie said, eyes wide. "Do something irresponsible? I can't imagine."

"What's that supposed to mean?"

"Only that in all the years I've known you, you've never done the slightest unexpected thing just for you. You're a rock, Jackson Tate, which is one of the things I love most about you."

"Eeeeuw!" Dillon made a face. "Mom loves Dad."

"I thought that was what you wanted?" Julie asked, tickling the boy's belly.

"It is," he admitted, squirming at her slightest touch, "but I don't want to hear you talking about it and stuff. That's just gross."

"To save you from dying of grossness," she teased, "from now on, I promise only to tell your father I love him in private, okay?"

"Okay," he said. Dillon looked at Jackson. "Plus, I'm really super glad you're not dating Ella like Owen told me." Pointing to his mom's bowl, Dillon asked, "Are you gonna eat that? Because if you're not, I will." He lunged for a cracker.

"Hold on there, sport," Jackson said, catching his boy about his waist, and hefting him off the bed and onto his feet. "I've already got a plate for you set up on the kitchen table."

"Aw, man. How come I can't eat with Mom in bed?"

"Because Mom's sick, and she doesn't need you dribbling

noodles all over her." Not to mention, tossing out any more conversational bombs about Ella.

"But—"

"You know what?" Julie said, easing her legs out from under the floral comforter. "I'm feeling a little better. How about we all eat downstairs?"

Ordinarily, Jackson wouldn't have minded, but seeing how he'd been planning to have his big talk with Dillon about his true feelings for Ella, he wished his ex would stay put.

"I DON'T KNOW why you gotta be mad at me," Owen complained after telling Ella the whole story of what had happened at the school sale. "It wasn't my fault that weird lady almost stole Rose."

"Again," Ella said, thrilled that the infant in question had finally fallen asleep in her crib, "I'm not mad, sweetie, just frustrated. What if the woman who held her was her mother? Right now, we're calling Sheriff Hank, and I want you to tell him exactly what you told me."

"Okay," he said, "but if I end up in the big house, I want you to come with me."

"I'll go," Oliver volunteered.

Ella rolled her eyes.

Two hours later, Hank had come and gone—having decided he'd rather speak with Owen in person than on the phone. Hank confided to Ella after the boys had gone to their rooms that, with Owen's sketchy description of the woman, the lead wasn't much to go on, but that he would ask some of the parents who had been at the sale if they'd seen the crying woman. He also requested that Ella attend the next school function with Rose. Hank would go too in hopes that the mystery woman would show again.

"I hope not." Just thinking about the last time her boys vanished took ten years off her life. "I'd die if you ran away again, and I don't want Owen to go, either."

"But Dad says to always be a man of my word." *He's one to talk!*

"In this case, I think it'll be all right if you break your word." She kissed his forehead. "Besides, you didn't really promise you'd run away, just mentioned it. So I don't think it counts."

After tucking the boys in for the night and cleaning the kitchen, Ella sat in the living room, nursing a mug of chamomile tea and rocking Rose.

"I can't even remember what life was like without you," she said to the tiny creature, tracing her perfect fingers and toes. "Somewhere out there, I'm guessing your mom is sorely missing you."

Ella couldn't fathom the courage it must have taken for the infant's mom to give her away. As much as she loved her sons, no force—human or nature—could ever pry her from them. True, Rose's mom could've given her away for selfish reasons, but Ella preferred to think her action had been that of a *selfless* person. A person who knew she couldn't give the infant adequate care, so she'd trusted her upbringing to another.

Ella had given a lot of thought to the fact that Rose's mom had to have been somewhat familiar with the park—or, at least the boys' playing habits—to have known when to safely leave the baby. Did Rose's mom know her? Had she maybe even been a patient? A sibling of a patient?

"You are quite the mystery," Ella said to the infant, who'd opened her big blue eyes. The baby held up her head just enough to stare. "Nicely done. You're growing up on me."

It was such fun sharing the baby girl with Jackson. How wonderful it would be to share the highs and lows of parenting full-time. Even when she and Todd had still been married, he'd always been somewhat of an absentee father. In his own way, she supposed he cared, but he'd never been the overly demonstrative type, acting as if hugs were billed by the second.

Having gotten to know Jackson, Ella envied Julie. Jackson was a wonderful father. He'd probably been an equally fantastic husband. Not the type to shower a woman with expensive gifts, but gifts far more precious. He'd give of his time. Affection. Laughter.

Leaning her head back, closing her eyes, she recalled that morning when she'd rested her head on his back. He'd felt so solid beneath her cheek. As if he had the strength to bear anything life threw his way. That's what he physically felt like, but emotionally, she feared he might break. Question was, when—if— that happened, would he turn to Julie for solace, or her?

"Yo, DUDE," Vince Calivaris called out to Jackson while they were headed back to the station Friday morning from what had turned out to be a bogus 4:00 a.m. call. "You totally just drove past the Bat Cave."

"Crap," Jackson mumbled under his breath. "Sorry about that."

At this hour, the four-lane city street the station was housed on was deserted, so he did a U-turn, quickly enough righting his mistake.

"No sweat, man."

They were back in the station house's gray-and-black dining room, downing Captain Crunch, when Calivaris asked, "What had you so deep in thought you forgot where we live?"

"You got a few days?" Jackson asked around a mouthful.

"At least till our shift ends. Spill."

Jackson told his friend the highlights, and by the time he'd

Run. Run!

Heart pounding, she weighed her options. If she did take her baby, she'd be so happy, but what then? She had only about a hundred bucks in her purse. That wouldn't get her very far. She didn't even have a diaper bag for the infant. And what would she feed her, as her milk had dried up long ago.

"Do I know you?" Owen asked. "You look kinda familiar."

"No," she said hastily, knowing the right thing to do would be to give the baby back, especially since she didn't even have enough money to feed her. "D-does she have a name?"

"We call her Rose, 'cause she's so pretty—like a rose."

"That's a beautiful name," she said with a sniffle, cradling the infant, tracing her eyebrows, her nose. Committing her every feature to memory since it seemed unlikely she'd get the opportunity to hold Rose again.

"Can I have her back?" Owen asked. "She's kinda mine."

No, she isn't.

It took every ounce of strength she had to return Rose to Owen's waiting arms. Because she loved her baby so much, and knew she couldn't care for her in the way she deserved, she tearfully handed over her baby, then vanished into the crowd, no longer trying to hold back her tears.

Torture.

The afternoon had been pure torture—at least as far as Ella was concerned. Standing around in hot sun, dealing with cranky bargain hunters intent on getting glassware for a nickel instead of a dime had been no biggie. Seeing Julie leading Jackson and Dillon around like her own personal sheep had tested her patience worse than parents who failed to bring their kids in for their annual immunizations.

Loading leftover toys and clothes into boxes to be delivered to a local charity, she tried not looking toward the happy family. Why hadn't they all just gone home to install their stupid crystal doorknobs? Why had they hung around helping when they weren't wanted?

"It's sure nice having Julie back, huh?" Marcia Jenkins strolled up, a boxful of paperbacks in her arms. "She's always been such a great asset to our PTA. We all hated seeing her go. She mentioned she and Jackson are getting remarried, but I thought you were dating him, Ella?"

"Nope," Ella said in as breezy a tone as possible. "We're just friends." Was Marcia purposely being cruel? Surely she'd known all that garbage Jackson had spouted about Rose being their *love child* had been a joke?

"Then why have you been upset all day?"

"Excuse me?" Now the woman had gone too far. "For your information, I've been in a wonderful mood—not that it's any of your business."

"Touchy, touchy," Marcia said. "Maybe someone's feeling more than friendly toward a certain child's father and Mr. Jealousy has decided to bite?"

"Marcia," Ella said, crowning her box with a neatly folded stack of T-shirts, "as far as I'm concerned, *you* can bite me."

Not giving the woman the satisfaction of looking back, Ella ignored Marcia when she called out, "I'm reporting you for that! We don't take kindly to rude behavior!"

Trembling, Ella gathered up Rose and the boys and high-tailed it to her minivan.

"Mo-om," Owen complained, climbing into the third-row seat. "I'm not ready to go. Me and Wally were playing tag."

"Get in the car," Ella said, not in the mood for whining. She made quick work of taking Rose from him, then settled her in her car seat, making sure the restraints were fastened

On autopilot, she picked up the phone, not only wanting to hear Jackson's voice, but to tell him about the possible break in their search for Rose's mom.

"Hello?" a woman asked.

"Ah, yes, may I please speak with Jackson?" Waiting for him to pick up, Ella bit her lower lip hard enough to draw coppery-tasting blood. Having already lost one man to another woman and knowing Julie was sleeping in the same house, Ella was unnerved. She trusted Jackson, but then she'd trusted Todd, too.

"This is Jackson," he eventually said.

"Sorry to bother you. Is Julie there?"

"Uh-huh." Judging by his cooler than usual tone, his ex was listening.

"I won't keep you, then." She briefly explained what had transpired in regard to Rose, then said, "Sorry again to have bothered you. I didn't mean to interrupt your night."

"You don't have to be sorry," he said. "Call any time."

After saying brief goodbyes, Ella knew she should go to bed, but with rain still hammering the roof and lightning strobing eerie shadows onto her moss-colored bedroom walls, sleep wouldn't come.

The only things that did come were memories of how awkward things had been between her and Jackson both tonight and that morning. He'd sounded stiff, as if he couldn't say what he'd wanted because Julie had been in the room. But if he truly meant what he'd said about irrevocably ending things with his ex, it shouldn't have mattered if she hovered. He was a grown man, able to say and feel whatever he wanted. Unless, maybe Dillon had also been present? In which case, she understood why Jackson would have had to be careful.

Whereas Ella had been fully confident of her decision to embark on a relationship with him, now she wasn't so sure.

What if he was having doubts? What if, in nursing Julie through even a simple cold, he realized he still loved her? What if Dillon had gotten through to him, convincing him that getting their family back together was the right thing to do?

Running her fingers into the hair at her temples, Ella groaned. The worst question of all was the one that had nagged her from the start. What if in getting together with Jackson, she was responsible for breaking Dillon's heart?

"WHAT DID ELLA WANT?" Julie asked when Jackson hung up the phone.

"Nothing much," Jackson said, not wanting to get into his newfound feelings for Ella with Dillon in the room. They were playing Monopoly at the kitchen table, munching popcorn, laughing: in general, having a surprisingly good time. But then Ella had called, in a sense bringing the outside world in.

"Tell me." Julie shifted in her chair to face him where he stood at the wall-mounted phone.

"It's your turn, Dad."

"Just a sec, bud." To Julie, he said, "She told me about a possible lead in finding Rose's mother."

"That's great," she straightened her play money. "Unless you were wanting to put your hat in the ring for adopting the baby?"

He remained silent.

"Were you?"

"I'd be lying if I said I hadn't at least thought about it." He stuck his hands in his pockets.

"I think we should adopt Rose, Dad. I always wanted a baby sister."

"It's not that simple." Jackson rejoined Julie and Dillon at the table. "Even if we wanted to adopt her, there's a lot of red tape." He and Ella would no doubt spend days in front of an attorney.

"You forget," Julie said, sipping from a can of Sprite, "you happen to be related to someone intimately acquainted with all manner of red tape and how to blast through it." She winked. Then she sighed wistfully. "Holding that sweet baby in my arms made me realize how much I've been yearning for another child. Rose will be very happy here with us."

Gulping, Jackson realized the error in his thinking. Classic Julie. She hadn't been offering to help him and Ella, but herself. Her utter lack of humility was a quality he'd alternately loved and hated. If she set her mind to it, she could pull off damn near anything—except resuscitating their marriage.

"JULIE, HI." It was Saturday morning, and Ella had wanted to dodge down the cereal aisle to avoid Jackson's ex, but she hadn't been quick enough. Rose was in her carrier, kicking air, and the twins were up front with six quarters, riding the bucking-elephant concession at the front of the store. "Feeling better?"

"Much, thank you. Last night, Jackson's mom made me her homemade chicken soup. It's a miracle cure."

"Mmm…I'll bet." Ella gripped the shopping cart's handle so tightly, her knuckles shone white.

"I'd forgotten how cute she is," Julie said, tickling Rose's tummy. "Jackson said there's been a lead in finding her mom."

"Maybe. Nothing definite, but at least Hank now has a clue."

"Mom?" Dillon raced around an end cap piled high with canned green beans and corn. He carried a box of taco shells. "Oh, hey, Ms. Garvey. Hi, Rose." He kissed the baby's cheek.

"Hey, Dillon." Had it really been only a few weeks since the boy used to greet Ella with a hug?

Attention back to his mother, Dillon said, "Dad wants me to ask you what brand of salsa you want him to buy."

"Tell him the locally made one with the green donkey on the label."

"Okay. Thanks." Dillon tossed the taco shells in Julie's cart, then raced off in search of his dad.

"Having Mexican night?" Ella forced herself to ask, adjusting Rose's crooked ruffled collar.

"It's Jackson's father's birthday. We're hosting a family party, and Mexican food's his favorite. He also likes burgers on the grill, though, so we're having those, too."

"That's nice," Ella said, feeling like a schmuck for not having known. But then how could she? Until recently, she'd only known Jackson through Dillon. And lately, Dillon had avoided her like math homework. "I, um, hope you all have fun."

The two said their goodbyes, then Ella was off to the baby aisle for formula and diapers, pretending it didn't matter that her almost-fiancé was party shopping with his ex who wanted to be his future.

She zinged her cart around a corner only to face Jackson, standing in front of baby toys.

"Busted," he said with the grin that'd first made her love him. In his hands were Julie's salsa and a duck rattle. "Would you like this, gorgeous?" For Rose, he gave the rattle a shake. "Oh, now I know that was a smile," he said when Rose's eyes lit with curiosity and the corners of her mouth turned up.

"It does look like one," Ella murmured, itching to shake some sense into him. What kind of game was he playing? A major condition to her agreeing to explore a relationship with him was the fact that he'd promised to officially break things off with Julie. As it stood, she was starting to feel like a floozy "other" woman.

"Sorry I had to cut it short on the phone last night. After dinner, Julie and Dillon wanted to play Monopoly, and we were right in the middle of our game."

"I understand," she said, lying through her teeth. "Sounds fun."

"It was. If only for the hour we were at the kitchen table, it felt like old times."

"I'm glad for you." Gaze downcast, she rearranged a few boxes at the bottom of her cart.

"Oh, Ell," he said, glancing over his shoulder before drawing her into a hug. "I'm sorry. I didn't mean for that to come out sounding bad. Just because Julie and I managed to sit through a game without fighting doesn't change the way I feel about you."

"I—I know," she said.

"Do you?" Fingers under her chin, he forced her to meet his eyes. "I love you, Ell. Nothing's going to change that." His tender kiss proved the meaning behind his words.

"Dad!" Dillon charged around the corner with Ella's twins hot on his heels. "Can Owen and Oliver and Rose come to Grandpa's part—" All three boys fixed Ella and Jackson with cold, hard stares. "I hate you!" Dillon cried. "Both of you!"

Chapter Fourteen

"I knew this would happen," Ella said to Jackson, her boys chasing after their friend who'd run for the front of the store. "Now, what are we going to do?"

Two white-haired retirees glared at the running boys, shaking their heads in disapproval.

"*We* are going to do nothing," he said, heading after his son.

"But Jackson," she tried reasoning, grabbing hold of his arm, "this concerns us both."

"Not really," he said. "I'm the one who didn't tell Julie of our change in plans. I need to fix this."

"But—"

Fingers to her lips, he said, "Go on with your day as if nothing happened. I'll call you when everything's settled."

Ella wasn't planning on holding her breath.

JACKSON FOUND HIS SON holed up in an abandoned shopping cart in the floral section of the store. He sat hunched over with his arms around his knees.

Owen and Oliver stood nearby, looking as though they weren't sure what to do.

Jackson suggested, "How about you two go find your mom?"

"You're not our dad," Oliver said, making a face.

"You're right," Jackson said, "but seeing how long I've known you, Oliver Garvey, I'm pretty darned close, so how about knocking off the sass?"

"Why were you kissing my mom?"

"Yeah," Owen piped in. "She's my mom, too."

Sighing, rubbing his jaw, Jackson said, "Your mom is a wonderful woman. I like her a lot."

"*We* like her *more,*" Owen said. "And I thought you were getting married to Dillon's mom. Even I know that means you kissing my mom is *cheating.*"

Counting to ten in his head, Jackson realized the time had come for him and Ella to sit down together with their broods and tell them how it was. Somewhere along the line, all of the boys had gotten the idea into their thick little heads that where their parents were concerned, they called the shots.

"Owen, Oliver," Jackson said in his strongest I-mean-business tone, "we're going to talk lots more about this later. But now, find your mother."

When both boys stood staring, Jackson added, *"Go."*

After a last slit-eyed glare, the twins scampered off.

"Now to deal with you," Jackson said under his breath.

"Go away," his son said with the vehemence of a striking rattler. "I hate you!"

"That's enough with the hate." Jackson plucked his kid from the cart.

"There you are," Julie said, rounding the corner with enough groceries to last a month. "What's wrong with the Garvey twins? They looked upset. Come to think of it, so did Ella."

"I'm sure they're fine," Jackson said between gritted teeth. "Let's pay for this stuff and go."

"Dad's lying," Dillon said, stabbing him with a defiant

stare. "Owen and Oliver are mad 'cause we caught their mom kissing Dad."

A myriad of emotions crossed Julie's face. Betrayal. Hurt. Anger. "Jackson? Is that true?"

He nodded. "Can we please get out of here? I'd like to discuss this in private."

"Of course," she said, having instantly regained her usual cool demeanor.

IN THE KITCHEN, groceries put away and their son safely out of earshot upstairs in his room, Jackson perched on a counter bar stool. "I haven't been entirely straight with you. And for that, I'm sorry."

"It's okay," she said with a faint smile. "Guess after what I did to you and Dillon, I've got whatever you can dish out coming."

"This isn't about revenge, Jules. You know that's not my style."

She nodded.

"I'm in love with Ella."

"You love her?" She was struck by a sudden coughing fit. "Jackson, you hardly know the woman."

"That's not true," he said, staring into the sun-dappled backyard. "She's been a second mom to Dillon for years."

"That's to our son—not you." She went to him, easing her arms around his neck. "Look, I get the whole fact that it's been two long years since you've been with a woman. You're a man and men have—" she blushed "—needs. Honey, think about it. Are you confusing those physical cravings for real, heart-felt emotion? The kind it takes years to forge?" Cupping his cheek, she admitted, "I like Ella. She's always been amazing with our son. I'll be the first to admit that the two of you are probably well suited, but that doesn't mean you should run off and elope. Look at what one kiss has done to our son. Above anyone on the planet, he adores you, Jackson, yet now he won't even look you in the eyes, let alone speak to you. Are you honestly willing to give up your very own son for a fling?"

Tensing beneath her touch, he said, "What I feel for Ella is more than a random fling."

"Of course it is. I'm not trying to discount your emotions. All I'm saying is don't jump into anything with so much at stake. I'll be the first to admit that after what I pulled in leaving, I don't deserve you, but that doesn't mean I don't still love you. That I don't still have a stake in our son's life. Above all, I want Dillon to be happy, and if that means you and I getting back together, Jackson, you have to agree we owe it to him to try."

"Sure," he said, using the heels of his hands to rub stinging eyes. What had led him to this place? How did he know if he truly did love Ella heart and soul, or if as Julie had suggested, his attraction for her was purely physical?

"If you'd like, why don't you invite Ella, Rose and the twins to your father's party tonight. See how she fits in with your family."

"That's no good," he said. "Dillon would pitch a fit."

"You let me handle Dillon," she said, patting Jackson's knee. "You just call Ella and let her know I bear no ill will toward her, and that she's welcome in our home."

"Julie…" Rubbing his jaw, he looked to the ceiling and sighed. "I love Ella. This fantasy you have of us getting back together is just that. A fantasy. I'm sorry, but I just don't feel—"

"Shh…" Julie's smile struck him as inappropriately bright. "You call Ella. I'll handle the rest."

"HAVE YOU LOST YOUR ever-loving mind?" Ella asked Jackson, hands on her hips. It was a gorgeous day, bright and sunny and she'd been on her knees in the front yard, weeding the flowerbed that wrapped around the porch. The gentle hum of insects and the neighbor's swishing sprinkler made it sound more like a lazy summer afternoon than spring. As idyllic as the yard looked, she couldn't have looked worse, wearing battered denim overalls and a paint-stained white T-shirt. "Why in the world would I want to come to a family dinner hosted by your ex-wife?"

"Because I asked?" he said, casting her a sweet smile.

"Nice try, Romeo, but I think I'll pass."

"Come on…" He slipped his arms around her waist. "I promise, Julie's one-hundred-percent okay with this. In fact, inviting you was her idea. I flat out told her I love you, and she said she didn't blame me for falling for you."

Ella laughed. "Now I know you're a few peaches shy of a bushel."

"Seriously. She said she'd even talk to Dillon about cutting you some slack."

"Correct me if I'm wrong," Ella said, backing away to remove her dirt-covered garden gloves, "but does any of this seem the slightest bit odd to you?"

"How so?"

"By her own admission, Julie wants you back, correct?"

"Yes." He shifted his weight from one leg to the other. "But what does that have to do with us?"

"She's playing head games with you, Jackson. She's one of the top criminal attorneys in the state. Hell—maybe even the whole country. Clients pay her truckloads of cash to get them out of whatever jam they happen to be in. That said, do you honestly think kindhearted you stands a chance of getting your way against a snake like her?"

"You're calling the mother of my child a snake?" A muscle popping in his jaw, he said, "That's pretty low, Ella, when all along, you wanted me to at least try getting back together with her. Now you accuse her of trying to manipulate me? And not only that, but you apparently think I'm simpleminded enough to fall for any mind tricks she throws my way?"

"I didn't say that. All I—"

He kicked a clump of dirt. "You've said enough. Come tonight or don't. At the moment, I really don't care."

"Jackson, don't leave angry," she said, catching up to him at the end of the drive. "I'm sorry if I hit a nerve in regard to Julie's motives. But I'd be lying if I told you I don't smell a rat. Women don't just willingly turn over men they supposedly love to another woman."

"You did." He refused to meet her gaze.

"How so?"

"Back before you agreed to enter into a relationship with me, you were all too willing to give me back to Julie."

A harsh laugh escaped Ella's lips. "Give you back? You're not mine to give. I don't own you. I don't expect anything from you other than mutual respect and truth. If you feel staying with Julie is the right thing for you and Dillon, then by all means, that's what you should do. Yes, I love you, but not enough to have you feeling bitter toward me for the rest of our lives over me having somehow stolen you from your first love."

"I'm sorry…" He crushed her with a hug. "It's been an emotional couple of days."

"I understand." Holding him every bit as tightly, never wanting to let go, she said, "Dealing with Dillon has got to be rough. Personally, I was thrilled when my two ran off down the block to play at someone else's house for a while."

Shaking his head, he admitted, "I'm out of my element here. I feel like I'm losing control of my own kid and it's scary."

"All he needs is love, then he'll come around." The words were easy enough to say. Ella just prayed her prediction of Dillon's behavior would come true.

"As a personal favor to me," Jackson said, sweeping stray hair from in front of her eyes. "Come tonight. I'm not sure that you've ever met my parents."

"Once," she said, stooping to pick a dandelion from the lawn, "at a neighborhood block party, but it's been a while."

"They'll love you as much as I do."

"But since we're doling out favors," Ella said with a heavy heart, "I need you to do me one, as well."

"Name it." He took the flower, tucking it behind her right ear.

"Don't tell them we're an item. Until we get all of our kids firmly on our side, I'd just as soon keep our romance on the down-low."

"Deal." After sealing their agreement with a soft, sweet kiss, he headed back to his house, and she headed back to her gardening.

Was it possible to lose twenty pounds in an afternoon without hacking off a limb? Outlook doubtful. But if she wanted to wear anything other than sweats for tonight's party, she at least needed to try.

"YOU'RE NOT GOING to kiss him again, are you?" Oliver asked on the walk to Jackson and Dillon's home. Ordinarily, Ella would've driven, but seeing how her bathroom scale said she still had nineteen and three-quarter pounds to lose, she figured the workout couldn't hurt.

"That's none of your business," she told her eldest son. "And I'd appreciate it if you at least try being polite to Jackson tonight. He likes you two very much."

Owen piped in with, "He didn't seem like he liked us this morning when he yelled at us."

"When did he yell at you?"

"At the grocery store. He told us to 'knock off the sass.'"

"Oliver," she asked, shifting the heavy casserole dish she carried from one arm to the other, "is that true?"

"I guess," he said, popping a wheelie with Rose's stroller, "but we were kinda mean to him."

"Stop doing that with the baby," she scolded before asking, "What did you do?" She stepped over a broken section of sidewalk.

"Told him he was a cheater 'cause he was marrying Dillon's mom, but kissing you."

Ella's stomach was already in a bad way, but that little snippet made her intestines seize.

"I hate Dawn," Oliver admitted, "because she cheated with Dad. I don't want you to be a cheater, too."

"Boys," she said, setting the casserole on Elda Loenstein's low rock wall. "One thing you need to know about me and Jackson is that while yes, Dillon's mom would like to get back together with him one day, they aren't a couple now. He's single. Just like me. Do you understand that? Do you guys get the fact that neither one of us is cheating?"

"I guess," Oliver said. "But I still don't like him."

"How can you say that? Ever since your dad left, Jackson's the one who's taken you fishing and played catch with you and let you camp out in his backyard."

"But he kissed you," Owen interjected, swinging the decorated bag filled with candy for Jackson's dad. "Only *we're* allowed to kiss you."

Sighing, Ella didn't know where to begin. How did she explain to eight-year-olds that their hugs and kisses were no longer enough? To say such a thing would break their hearts. Yet, lately, since Jackson had come into her life, she'd felt as though if he didn't stay in her life, hers would be the heart that was broken.

Across the street, Miles Polk started up his mower. The rush of pollen and dust made Owen sneeze.

"God bless you," she said to her youngest, ruffling his fine hair. "We'd better get going, huh?"

"I'm not going anywhere," Owen said, "till you promise you're not going to do any more kissing."

"Happy birthday, Mr. Tate."

Jackson took Rose from her stroller while Ella introduced herself to his father, then his mother.

"Dillon has told us so much about you," his bouffant-coifed mother said. "I know we have to have met at some point or another."

"We have," Ella said with a gracious smile, shaking both of their hands. "It's been at least five years, though."

"Well, it's good to see you again."

"Here's your present," Owen said, thrusting the bag at Jackson's dad. "It's lots of little candy bars. Snickers and stuff."

"Thank you." The birthday boy helped himself to a Reese's Peanut Butter Cup.

"Walter…" his wife warned. "Your cholesterol."

"I'm sorry," Ella said, "had I known, I would have gotten you a nice coffee table book."

"It's all right," Jackson's mother assured Ella. "His number's not all that high, but you can never be too careful."

"Ella, you made it," Julie said, sailing in from the kitchen. She wore an expensive-looking pink sundress, over which she'd tied a black-and-white gingham apron. "Hey, guys," she said to the twins. "Dillon's out back playing Frisbee with his cousins."

"Rick and Vicky?" Owen asked.

Oliver groaned. "Vicky's mean. She tried to put lipstick on me last time she was here."

"Come on," Jackson said, his hand on Oliver's back. "I'll take you out and tell Vicky to cool it with her makeup." The girl was five and had already decided on a career in high fashion.

"I'll go by myself," Oliver said, scrunching out from under Jackson's touch.

"Suit yourself," Jackson said, "but if she nails you with her new mascara, don't come cryin' to me."

"What's mask-scara?" Owen asked.

"Superscary stuff," Jackson said. "Come on, I want to see what my brother's up to."

Jackson had never been close with his older brother, Liam. Ten years his senior, by the time Jackson had been able to drive, Liam had already bought a home and car, and was on his way to getting married. Unfortunately, he was now divorced due to a case of irreconcilable differences. This was one of the rare times Liam got to be with his children. He had joint custody, but only had them one weekend per month because his ex lived a couple of hundred miles away.

"How's it going?" Jackson asked his brother out on the patio.

Liam was flipping burgers. The deliciously smoky scent of beef had Jackson's stomach growling. Julie had tackled the Mexican portion of the meal with an enchilada casserole and tacos. "Everything's just about done," he said before turning the kids' hot dogs.

"Thanks for handling this," Jackson said. "Mom's had me inside, lecturing me on how to put some special rinsing stuff in the dishwasher."

Laughing, Liam said, "I feel your pain, bro. She gave me the same lecture a couple of years back. Just roll with it. It makes her feel important to make us feel like idiots."

"I think you're right."

Liam added American cheese slices to the burgers, then said, "While I've got you to myself, I wanted to tell you how happy I am about you and Julie getting back together."

"Where'd you hear that?" Jackson asked.

"Dillon. He's damned excited about getting his mom back." Shaking his head, Liam said, "I never did understand Julie's leaving. Guess she finally came to her senses. I know I'd give anything for a second chance with Barb. Divorce is an ugly, ugly thing."

"Yeah," Jackson said, "only I'm not so sure I want to take Julie up on her offer to move back. She hurt me. Bad."

"See those kids over there?" Liam nodded toward his two. "Every time I have to leave them, I feel like a piece of me is dying. I know you didn't ask for my advice, but I'm giving it to you anyway. Do whatever it takes to get—and keep—Julie in your and Dillon's lives. She's an amazing lawyer with connections that'd make your head spin. If she wanted to take Dillon from you, it'd be a snap."

"She wouldn't do that," Jackson said, using the grill lighter to ignite citronella candles.

"You sure? Like, bet-on-Dillon's-life sure?"

"That's nuts."

"Is it? I'm living proof, man, that the old saying about hell and a scorned woman is one-hundred-percent true."

"There you are," Julie said, appearing with a clean plate for the hot dogs and burgers. "Everything almost done?"

"Yep," Liam said, settling a companionable arm about her slim shoulders, then kissing her cheek. "It's good having you back, sis. I've missed you."

"Liar," she teased. "All you've missed are my potato salad and brownies."

"Guilty," he said with a wince. "Speaking of which, we are having both tonight, right?"

"Right." His roundabout compliment to Julie's two signature dishes earned Liam an affectionate return kiss. "I've missed you, too."

Jackson had forgotten how well Liam and Julie had gotten along. As a hardcore stockbroker, Liam's type-A personality was closer to Julie's than Jackson's had ever been.

"Need a hand?" All three adults already on the patio looked at Ella.

Vicky came running over and asked, "Who are you?"

"I'm Ella," she said, "and you must be one of Dillon's cousins."

"Uh-huh," the little girl said. "Want me to do your makeup?" From her pink backpack, she pulled an amazingly complete makeup kit.

"Thank you so much," Ella said. "I could probably use a touch-up on my blush."

"Sit there," Vicky commanded, never having been shy and pointing to the chaise where Ella and Jackson had kissed the night she'd been here for dinner. Jackson caught her stare. Did she remember?

Her hastily ducked gaze and cheeks rosy red without the help of blush told him she did.

"Be kind, Miss Vicky," Liam warned, as he and Julie turned to talk privately.

"I *will*," she said, her pout making her look mortally wounded that her dad didn't have complete faith in her talent.

"Make me gorgeous," Ella requested.

Surreptitiously kissing the top of Ella's head, Jackson said in a for-her-ears-only tone, "You don't need much help in that department."

"Aren't *you* a charmer?" Ella glanced up, a twinkle in her eyes.

"I try."

"Quit talking!" The makeup artist hit Jackson with one of her brushes.

"Ouch. What are you hitting me for?"

Vicky fisted her hands on her hips. "Because you keep making google eyes at her, and I'm trying to make her pretty."

Lord, was he that obvious? Luckily, Liam was busy chatting up Julie and hadn't heard his daughter. "Since I'm not wanted at the beauty parlor, I'm going to check on my folks. You going to be all right?" He brushed Ella's shoulder, her skin as soft as warm silk.

"I'll be fine," she said, grinning up at him. "I can tell I'm in expert hands."

Liam, carrying the plate of burgers and hot dogs, followed Jackson inside.

They were alone in the kitchen when Liam asked, "What in Sam Hill do you think you're doing?"

"Excuse me?" Jackson tensed.

"Ella. You've got a thing for her, don't you? Here you've

got a once-in-a-lifetime shot at the perfect do-over, and you're shooting it straight to hell."

"Anyone ever tell you to mind your own business?" Turning his back on his brother, Jackson grabbed the ketchup, mustard and mayo from the fridge.

"I'd love to, but I'm worried about you doing the right thing. Admittedly, Doc Ella's pretty and smart and seems nice enough, but we're talking Julie. She used to be everything to you. And then there's Dillon. He's wholly invested in you and Julie getting back together. If that doesn't happen, can you even imagine what that's going to do to him?"

Trying to keep as tight a hold on his emotions as he had on the mayo jar, Jackson said, "Get this straight. I love my boy. I'd do anything to make Dillon happy."

"If you truly mean that," Liam said, slamming the plate of burgers on the counter before opening a sack of buns, "publicly announce you and Julie are getting back together. Nothing would make Dad happier."

Chapter Fifteen

Ella closed her eyes while Jackson's niece applied eye shadow. Truth be told, she was a tad spooked about what she might end up looking like, especially since Julie was looking her glamorous best. But the kid lover in Ella couldn't turn down an adorable little girl's request.

"You need blush," Vicky said. "Lots and lots and *lots* of blush."

"Thank you," Ella said, laughing. "But maybe you should leave off one of the *lots?*"

"No," the girl said with a firm shake of her head.

"Vicky…" Jackson's brother warned, stepping back outside.

"What, Daddy? I'm making her—what was your name again?"

"Ella."

"Yeah, I knew that was it." The child waved her purple lipstick. "Okay, now pucker up, Ella, like you're gonna kiss Uncle Jack."

"Vicky," Liam said, a harsh edge to his voice. "That's enough. Get inside and wash up for dinner."

When the girl had left, Ella rose. "Is everything all right?"

"Peachy." His condemning stare spoke volumes. Did he

suspect she and his brother were secretly an item? If so, would it be safe to assume he disapproved? "By the way, dinner's ready."

Julie had set a lovely table in the dining room. With the leaves in, the gleaming cherry table sat the whole crowd comfortably. Crystal wineglasses caught the low-hanging chandelier's dim light, and flickering candles completed a romantic setting that seemed incongruous to the evening's picnic and fiesta fare. Three silver vases held fragrant white roses and lilies with ivy draping the sides. The setting was completed by soft classical music Ella didn't recognize, but enjoyed.

"Jules, my girl," Jackson's father said, "I'd forgotten what a fine spread you put on. Welcome back to the family, sweetheart."

"Thank you, Dad." Julie raised her glass. "To Walter, may each birthday surprise top the last. Cheers."

"Cheers," all gathered said, raising their glasses as well.

Down at the kids' end of the table, where Ella's name card had been located, everyone drank sparkling cider instead of the champagne the grown-ups had been served. Ella had asked for bubbly, but since Jackson's parents weren't big drinkers, Julie had only purchased one bottle. By the time she'd reached Ella's glass, only a few drops had come out.

Rose was the lucky one, zonked out in her carrier in a quiet corner of the living room.

"I didn't want to sit by you," Dillon whispered for Ella's ears only. "My mom made me, and she said I have to be nice."

"I thought we were friends," she said. "What happened?"

Ignoring her, he squirted a sea of ketchup onto his plate.

"Dillon?" she prodded while her boys were busy chatting with Rick. "Please, sweetie, talk to me."

"I. Don't. Want. To."

Okay...

"Vicky," Julie said, "you did a pretty job with Ella's makeup."

"Thanks." The girl beamed before biting into a hot dog smothered in mustard and relish.

Ella's stomach sank.

After Liam's downright hostile behavior toward her, she'd forgotten to check herself out in the powder room mirror before joining the others. Just how awful did she look? Convinced her complexion was now clownlike, when no one peered her way, she wiped her cheeks with her ivory cloth napkin.

"That was some town meeting the other night, wasn't it?" Walter asked, his plate piled high with Mexican food, and a burger poised at his lips.

"Honey, don't bring up such unpleasantness at the table," his wife admonished.

"It's okay, Dad," Jackson said. "It's your birthday. Let her rip."

After casting a victorious glance at his wife, Walter said, "I think I will."

"Wait," Ella interjected, "first, let me say I wholeheartedly agree with you in that the meeting was a sham. The fact that our illustrious city leaders want to demolish the Taggart Theater—one of the state's first—to make room for a car lot. Well…" She shook her head. "It's unconscionable. In fact—"

"Ell…" Jackson cleared his throat.

"Wait a sec," she said, "I'm just getting fired up. When I heard how the board was planning to vote, I—"

"Dorothy," Walter said, pushing back his chair and standing. "Get your purse. We're leaving."

"What's wrong?" Jackson's mother asked. "Is your acid indigestion flaring up?"

"*She's* what's wrong," Walter said, pointing down the table at Ella. "Young lady, that's not just any old car lot being proposed for that site, but mine. I enjoy a historic building as much as anyone in this town, but that particular building would cost millions to restore, and even then, feasibility studies have shown the likelihood of a space that size generating a working income is—" He clutched his chest, and Ella was instantly out of her chair.

"What's wrong?" she asked at his side, grabbing his wrist to take a pulse. "Is it your heart?"

"No, you silly woman. My heart's fine, but thanks to you, my stomach feels like it's on fire."

"Dad," Jackson said, on his feet, as well, "calm down. Ella didn't mean anything personal. She had no idea you're behind the—"

"It's okay," Ella said, fighting back tears. How had this night gone from bad to even worse? She'd known she should've stayed home. Why, why hadn't she listened to that inner voice telling her to steer clear of this cozy Tate family gathering? Especially when Julie had been involved. Trouble was, as much as Ella wanted to blame the night's horrors on Jackson's ex, the truth was she had no one but herself to blame. "I'll go. Walter, I'm sorry if my views upset you. Boys," she called to the twins. "Let's head home."

"I'll take you," Jackson said.

"No, Dad!" Dillon pushed back his chair so hard, it tipped, then ran to his father, tossing his arms around him. "I don't want you to go."

"Dillon…" Jackson looked to the ceiling before returning his son's affection.

"I'll run you home in Jackson's SUV," Liam said, already out of his chair. "You've got a baby seat, right?"

Jackson nodded. He glanced her way, then down to his son, still clinging to him. "Thanks, bro."

"No problem. Ready?" he asked Ella and her crew.

"Walter," Dorothy said, "the boys haven't even finished their dinner. You don't really want them to go, do you?"

Without saying a word, Walter sat back down and picked up his burger.

"I'm so sorry," Dorothy Tate said, bustling after Owen and Oliver, picking up their plates. "Let me just wrap these to go."

Ella tried hooking Jackson's gaze on her way past, but he didn't bite. Nice. Good to know he had her back.

"FOR WHAT IT'S WORTH," Liam said, carrying Rose and her carrier to Ella's front door, "Dad can sometimes be a real tool. He was in rare form tonight."

"It's okay," she said. "It's his birthday. He's entitled to have his own way."

"I could tell Jackson was torn."

"I said it's all good." Ella held out her arms for the baby. "The last thing I'd intended was to ruin your father's celebration."

"I know. We all know. Like I said, in his golden years, he's turned crusty."

Not trusting her voice past the lump in her throat, Ella nodded, while Liam handed over Rose. "Thanks again for the ride."

"No problem." She'd turned to go inside when he said, "There's ah, one more thing…"

"Yes?" Rose snuggled her head into the crook of Ella's neck. The loving gesture was much needed in light of Liam's narrowed gaze.

"I don't know what you and my brother have going, but you have to realize he has a lot at stake."

"With Julie, you mean?"

"And his son. Do you really want to be the woman who rips apart his perfect family?"

"Gee," she said, at the moment sick of the entire Tate clan, "maybe it's just me, but from the outside looking in, I'm guessing it was Julie's leaving that did the most damage to Jackson's marriage—not me."

By the time Liam had pulled out of her driveway, and she'd gone inside, Ella was shaking. How dare he make such an accusation? This whole night had been insane. Talk about multiple signs from above that she and Jackson were never meant to be…

"Mommy?" Owen stood at the base of the stairs.

"Yes, hon?" His cheeks were damp; he'd been crying.

"Why was Dillon's grandpa so mean to you?"

"Oh, sweetie," she said, sitting on the second stair, so she could hold Owen and Rose. "He was probably just upset about his presents. You know, like maybe he asked for a bike, but got boxers instead."

"How come Dillon didn't stop him? I thought he was our friend?"

"He is, sweetheart. Dillon's probably confused."

"About what?"

How did Ella explain what was wrong with a child when the grown-ups he looked to for role models had acted even more immaturely than any of his friends? When she next saw Jackson, she fully planned on giving him a piece of her mind. For a man who supposedly loved her, he sure had a funny way of showing it.

"YOUR FATHER seemed to have a nice time at his party, don't you think?" Though she still slept in the guest bedroom, Julie had made herself at home in the master bath. Seated on the bench in front of the vanity, she brushed her long hair, then put it in a ponytail for the night.

"Were you at the same party?" he asked, perching on the edge of the oversize soaking tub.

"That little spat with Ella was nothing." Dabbing cream under her eyes, she added, "I'll bet in the morning he sends her flowers to apologize."

Jackson shook his head. "When hell freezes over will my father change positions on this."

"Please don't take this the wrong way," she said, "but maybe it's best you found out now that Ella and your family don't exactly fit. I know your mom was furious when Ella's boys presented Walter with a sack full of candy. And Liam—"

"Knock it off." Jackson rose, shooting her a condemning stare. "What you're doing is awfully transparent. I thought you were above petty tactics like this."

"Tactics? Honey, all I did was try to play the role of a welcoming hostess. Any altercations your *girlfriend* found herself in were entirely of her own making."

"Ella's not my girlfriend, she's—"

"What?" Julie snapped, spinning around on the small, satin-covered bench. "Please, Jackson, tell me exactly what that woman is to you, other than a person trying to tear our family apart? Nobody likes her. Least of all, our son."

As much as Jackson wanted to rail against his ex for trash-talking Ella, the sad fact of the matter was that she was right. His family hadn't liked her. But had they even given her a chance? Liam had always had a soft spot for Julie, making him firmly in her camp. His dad had always been a bear—meaning, he didn't like anyone. As for his mother, she was from another era when women did as their husbands told them. A fact of life he now realized he'd never be able to change.

"Jackson," Julie said, voice soothing, "I'm sorry if tonight didn't go as you'd planned. Your dad's always been…" she made a face "…unpredictable."

"That's putting it politely."

She came to him, curving her fingers around his shoulders. "No matter what you decide in regard to Ella, you have to know I love you. I dearly love our son, as do you. Together again, we could set the world on fire." She kissed him— barely. Just grazing her lips against his.

"Julie…" Hadn't he made it clear the last time they'd spoken he had no intention of hooking back up?

"It's all right," she said, kissing him deeper. "I'm good with the fact that for the time being our reunion is one-sided. All I'm asking for, Jackson, is a chance. I can handle the fact that it might be a slim one. I can't handle that it may be nonexistent."

He was tired. So very freakin' tired of fighting her. His son. Most of all, his heart. Reuniting with Julie would be so easy. Make the vast majority of people in his life happy. He'd once loved Julie heart and soul. Who knew? Maybe, in time, he could grow to love her again?

An image of Ella flashed before his mind's eye. A knot of tension grew over how much he adored her now. But was that enough? Could he handle being as distant from Dillon as Liam was from his children? What if Julie did decide to fight for custody? Bottom line, Jackson would die before losing his son. A fact that didn't leave him a whole lot of options.

ELLA DEBATED whether to phone Jackson after the party, but decided against it. In regard to his not defending her against his father, she'd give him the benefit of the doubt. She was sometimes weird around her parents. Old relationship patterns died hard.

She'd tucked in the twins, then moved on to Rose who'd already been asleep for the better part of an hour, but that was all right, as Ella's sole purpose for being in the moonlit room was just to look at her. Drink her in: her perfect tiny fingers and toes, the elegant sweep of her eyelashes against chubby cheeks, the way her rosebud mouth suckled after every two or three exhalations.

Fitting her fingers to the crown of the infant's head, Ella realized with a frightening intensity just how much she'd grown to love the baby girl. Somewhere along the line, her feelings for Jackson and this wee one had intertwined until her adoration of both had grown to the point that she didn't know what she'd do without them. The secret prayer in her heart was that she'd never have to find out.

The phone rang.

Ella gave Rose's rump a pat before jogging to pick up the bedroom extension. Only, when she got there, the line was dead.

Checking the caller ID, she noticed Jackson had been on the other end of the line. Figuring he must've gotten disconnected, she sat on the edge of the bed, pulse pounding. Was he calling to apologize?

But the longer she waited, the longer the bedroom's silence closed in around her. The ticking of the alarm clock, the barking of the neighbor's basset hound, the drip from the shower faucet she'd been meaning to have fixed.

Ella woke eight hours later, still wearing her dress from the night before, Rose wailing in the adjoining nursery that had been the twins' before she'd taken it over.

"The baby's awake," Oliver said, hovering over the crib.

"Why didn't you pick her up?" Ella asked, rubbing sleep from her eyes.

He shrugged.

She shook her head.

Kids. Had it really only been the previous night she'd wondered what she'd do without them?

Ella changed Rose, then traipsed down to the kitchen to get

the baby and the boys fed. That task completed, she left Rose in Owen's hands, then dashed upstairs for a quick shower. Odds were, Jackson would be over bright and early to apologize and she wanted to look her best.

Wearing white capris and a pale-blue tank that showed off her tan, she'd blow-dried her hair and brushed it into soft waves, leaving it loose and flowing down her back. After adding a little makeup and cute white sandals, she practically skipped back downstairs. Laughing, she swept Rose from Owen's arms and twirled her around.

"What's wrong with you?" Oliver asked over a blaring Barney tape they hadn't watched in years. Ella hadn't even known they still had it.

"Not a thing," she said, kissing Rose's cheek. "Is it wrong for me to be happy?"

"I don't guess so." Oliver plopped back down on the cream-colored carpet, intent on watching the show.

"I thought Barney was only for babies?" she asked.

"It is," Owen said with a put-upon sigh, "but Rose likes it."

"Oh," Ella said with a nod. "Of course she does. You two are clever to have found that out. If you need me, I'll be in the kitchen."

"What're you doing, Mom?"

"I don't know about you guys, but I could use some home-made cookies."

When the sun-flooded kitchen smelled rich with the aroma of still-warm chocolate-chip-and-peanut-butter cookies, finally a knock sounded.

A glance in that direction showed Jackson standing behind the mullioned back door.

Although she had been excited at the thought of seeing him, tension now knotted her stomach. He was here to apologize, right? Because if he wasn't, she wasn't sure how to handle him. She'd be furious, but she was really more in the mood for kissing than fighting.

"Hey," he said, not waiting for her to open the door.

"Hey, yourself." As upset as she'd been the night before, seeing him again swelled her heart with love. Holding grudges had never been her strong suit, and this time was no different. He surely had his reasons for his abnormal behavior. Which was why he was here. To explain—and, of course, apologize.

Tossing her arms around his neck, she clutched him to her. He hugged her back, squeezing her almost uncomfortably tight.

"We need to talk."

"I know," she said. "I made cookies. Want ice cream to go with them?"

"You're too good to me," he said, voice raspy as he kissed her forehead instead of her lips.

"Nah… Just in the mood for sweets. Come on," she took his hand, leading him toward the stairs. "We'll talk in my room. It'll be more private. Then we'll eat."

"O-okay."

Upstairs, Ella sat on the foot of the bed, patting the empty spot beside her. "You know the real reason I invited you up here, don't you?"

"No."

She rolled her eyes. "I wanted to steal a few kisses out of sight of a certain set of twins."

Jackson remained silent, not meeting her gaze.

"Jackson, what's wrong?"

He cleared his throat and peered out the window with his hands tucked firmly into the front pockets of his jeans.

"Ell… Geez, where do I start?"

She again patted the bed.

"Thanks. But for this, I need to stand." He not only stood, but began to pace.

That nervous tension in her stomach? It worsened.

"Last night was a disaster."

"No kidding," she said with a biting laugh.

"But it did serve a purpose."

"Making me feel like crap had a *purpose?*" Though she had been feeling sentimental and forgiving, that last line left her just plain mad. "I'm ready for my apology, Jackson. *Now.*"

"I *am* sorry, Ell. I'm sorry for my father's boorish behavior. For my brother's and mother's and Julie's and Dillon's, but most of all, for mine. I should've defended you, but…"

"It's okay," she said, standing to hug him, letting him know she understood. Sort of. Lucky for him, he had a lifetime to make it up to her. As for his family, she supposed there were lots of tension-filled in-laws out there. She'd live through it. They all would, and be stronger for having done it.

"No, it's far from okay," he said, giving her a gentle nudge. "Ell, I came to some hard realizations last night. No—impossible realizations. The worst part is that all along, you were right. We have no business being together."

What? No, no, no… This speech couldn't be leading where she feared.

"Liam set me straight on so many things. Most importantly, that as a father, I have to put Dillon first."

"Of course you do," she said. "I'm not asking you for anything else."

"Don't you get it? To put him first means reuniting him with his mother."

She struggled for composure. "I've been telling you that for weeks. You were the one saying Dillon would get over it.

That he could still be close to Julie and to me. Make up your mind, Jackson. You can't have it both ways."

"No one knows that more than me," he said, raising his arms as if wanting to hold her, but he didn't. A good thing, seeing how she never wanted to see him again—let alone touch him. "Which is why I have to marry Julie. I have to. Please understand."

"I understand, all right," she said, turning her back on him to stare out the window. "I understand I was a fool ever to have trusted you."

"Don't say that," he begged, hovering behind her. "I do love you. I'll always love you. But as a father, I have to love my son more."

"I get that," she said, crossing her arms. "You've made your point clear.

"I never meant to hurt you."

"Please, go."

"Ell…"

"*Please,* Jackson." She squeezed her stinging eyes shut. "I understand, and there's nothing else left to say."

Chapter Sixteen

Friday night, five days after he'd broken things off with Ella, Jackson sat in the Key Elementary cafeteria, staring at three bingo cards. It was Pizza Bingo Night—another big fundraiser. Dillon sat to his left, alongside his mom. The kid hadn't stopped smiling since Julie had arrived just in time to pick him up from school.

Rose and Ella and a bunch of her PTA mom friends sat four tables over—the twins were with classmates. The stress of her proximity was about to do him in. Or was it the cloistering heat? The approximately eight thousand parents and kids crammed into the small space? Or maybe the stale pepperoni he'd downed with three of those pint-size kid cartons of milk? Regardless, he was in a bad way, and couldn't wait to get the heck out of there.

"You all right?" Julie asked, leaning past their son. "Your color's off."

"B-3," Farrah Benton from Channel Six Action News called out. Marcia Jenkins took great pride in landing local celebrities for this big event. "The next number is B-3."

"I'm good," he said, marking two of his cards.

"You don't look good." She only marked one of her cards. "Did the pizza make you sick? Because it sure made me sick."

"Yeah," he mumbled, wishing that was the extent of his problems. If only he had a crystal ball to tell him if he'd made the right decision. Looking at Dillon's bright eyes he had to believe he had. But the dread in the pit of his stomach every time he thought of spending the next fifty or so years with Julie was getting hard to bear. He loved her, but in a she-bore-my-child kind of way. When she'd left him and Dillon without a single thought about how badly something like that would hurt, his passionate love for her was over. The trauma their son had faced, and the many nights Jackson and Ella had held him while he'd cried had frozen the part of his heart once devoted to Julie.

Now, there was no going back.

He was trying though.

For Dillon's sake, no matter how bad it personally hurt, he had to make a new life with Julie work.

"I-17. Repeating, the next number is I-17."

Across the room, he caught Ella's gaze.

She hastily looked away.

"Hey, look!" Dillon cried, pointing to a tall, thin girl who stood against the rear wall. She had long, dark hair and wore faded jeans and a red T-shirt. At the moment, she was staring at Rose, who Ella had out of her carrier. The baby had fallen asleep, resting her head on Ella's shoulder. "That's the lady who cried holding Rose at the yard sale."

"You sure?" Jackson asked.

"Yep." Dillon nodded vigorously. "See that mole thingie next to her lips? Me and Owen think it looks like a—"

"Dillon," Julie scolded. "It's not nice to talk about people's appearances. Now, as your father asked, are you sure that's the lady? Because if it is, Daddy's friend wants to talk to her."

"It is," the boy said, bouncing on his seat. "Promise."

"Be right back," Jackson said. "I'm going to get Hank."

LOOKING AT her baby always made her want to cry. She should've been happy, knowing her baby was content, but it really just made her miss Rose all the more.

Many times she'd thought about what she'd do if she did get her baby back. She'd thought about taking Rose home to the farmhouse where she lived with her grandmother and dad. They'd be furious with her. Consumed with shame.

She knew even in coming here again, she was taking a risk of being caught, but that couldn't be helped. She had to see Rose just one more time. If only she could hold her. Tell how much she loved her, and—

"Excuse me, ma'am?"

She looked up to see a tall man standing beside her. Her first instinct was to run, but her heart beat so fast, she felt frozen in place.

"B-12," the glamorous bingo caller said with a Hollywood-white smile. "The next number is B-12."

"Ma'am, my name is Hank Norman, and I'm the local sheriff." He flashed a badge. "Would you mind stepping into the vestibule for a moment while I ask you a few questions?"

"Questions? A-about what?" she asked, gaze darting to Rose. "I—I haven't done anything wrong."

"That's what I'm here to find out."

She started to bolt out to the kitchen, but the sheriff was lightning fast, grabbing hold of her elbow, then jerking her around to face him. "Ouch," she cried. "You're hurting me."

"Sorry, ma'am. I'm afraid if you choose to run, the use of force to stop you can't be helped. Now, will you come with me peaceably, or would you like to make a scene?"

"I'll come," she said, "just please don't tell my daddy."

"ELLA?"

She looked up from her bingo cards only to face her worst nightmare. "Go away," she whispered to Jackson, shielding Rose. "You and I have nothing more to say."

"This isn't about us, but Rose. Hank's found her mother."

"O-67. The next number is 0-67."

Ella's blood ran cold.

No. She'd already lost the man she'd loved. Now she was losing her baby, as well? Yes, she knew—she'd always known—Rose wouldn't be hers, but lately, she'd begun to hope.

"Ella…" Jackson held out his hand to help her up from the cramped table. His words warm in her ear, he whispered, "Come with me. Hank's got Rose's mom out in the lobby."

Refusing to take Jackson's hand, Ella stiffly stood. Cradling Rose, she ignored Marcia Jenkins's stare, stoically leaving the cafeteria while the bingo game went on around her. The vast majority of the room was most likely oblivious to what was going on, but Ella couldn't help but feel that the few who did know were secretly glad to see her losing yet one more person from her life. Case in point, Julie, who'd left Dillon with a gang of his friends, and now hustled down the opposite side of the cafeteria, converging with them at the entrance.

"Ella," Julie said in hushed tones. "I heard, and I'm—"

"Save it," Ella said, in no mood for chitchat.

Hank stood by the school office, Principal Wood on his left and a scared-looking young girl on his right.

"Rose," the girl said, holding out her arms. "Please, can I hold my baby?"

The love on the girl's face was so intense, Ella didn't have the heart to refuse. "Here you go," she said. "Be careful of her head. She still needs support."

Upon taking Rose into her arms, the girl began to cry. Sob, really. "I—I've missed you so bad."

As much as Ella's heart was breaking for her own loss, the joy on the girl's face was contagious. This was the whole reason she'd volunteered to keep Rose in the first place, so that they'd have a shot at finding the infant's mom and reuniting them.

Reuniting them.

Ironic how that was the same reason she'd lost Jackson—so that he, Dillon and Julie could get back together.

Wishing to give the girl her privacy, Ella pulled Hank aside. "Tell me everything you know."

"The girl's name is Stacia Tabor. Her family belongs to the church out on Old Berry Road. I forget the name, but they're the kind of congregation that frowns upon unwed mothers. Apparently, she's been homeschooled, which is why we were unable to track her through school records."

"You're not going to press charges, are you?"

"I should," Hank said, gazing off to the school's main entrance.

In the cafeteria, an excited child hollered, "Bingo!"

The majority of the crowd moaned a resounding, *"Awwww."*

Ella asked Hank, "What does Stacia want to do in regard to Rose?"

"She wants you to raise her, but she's asked to be allowed to visit—which is why I don't see any point in hurting her further by prosecuting her."

Ella's heart momentarily swelled, but then she caught sight of Claire Donaldson, who'd been sitting with her second-grade class. Her expression was one of hope. She and her husband had tried so hard for a baby of their own, but so far had failed. Adopting Rose would bring them such joy. Ella had already been blessed with two healthy children. The right thing to do would be to give up Rose, but was she strong enough? Could her heart take it?

Claire approached. "Well?" she asked, eyes bright with excited apprehension. "Does Rose's mother know what she wants to do?"

Swallowing hard, Ella nodded, forcing a bright smile. "Nothing's official, but according to Hank, she doesn't want her family to know she even had a baby. She asked if I'd like to keep Rose, but as much as I adore her, raising an infant on top of my two, plus work at the clinic, is all getting to be too much. I want you and Jeremy to have her."

"Oh—oh, Ella…" Tearing up, Claire held trembling hands over her mouth. "How can I—we—ever thank you?"

"You already did," Ella said, drawing her into a hug.

Noting that Rose's mother had calmed, Ella went to her. "Leaving your baby alone in the park was very dangerous."

"I—I know," the girl said. "But I knew your boys from working at their day care. I knew when they usually went to the park, and I didn't leave my baby there until I knew she'd be found right away. Only, I didn't just want her found by anyone, but by a good loving family—like yours. Thank you for taking such good care of her."

"You're welcome," Ella said. "I've grown to love your baby very much, and Hank said you'd like me to keep on raising her?"

"If that's all right? Rose seems happy with you and your boys. And aren't you and Dillon Tate's dad getting together?"

Pain ripped through Ella, but not the kind medical science had a clue how to fix. A glance in Jackson's direction showed him side-by-side with Julie, a grim expression on his face. There was so much Ella wanted to share with him in regard to Rose, but what was the point? He knew the gist of how things had turned out.

"Come on," Ella said, putting her broken heart out of her mind while drawing Stacia and Rose over to Claire. "There's someone I'd like you ladies to meet."

"THAT SURE WAS A NICE moment between Rose and her mom, wasn't it?" Saturday morning, Julie stood on a ladder in the entry hall, painting the formerly pale-blue walls gray. Jackson hated it.

"Yeah," he said.

"What's the matter? Weren't you glad to finally solve the mystery of who is Rose's mother?"

"Sure." He knelt to swipe a paint drip from the hardwood floor.

"Then why so glum?"

"I'm not sure," he admitted, sitting hard on the stairs.

"Let me guess…" Resting her paintbrush on the paint can's lip, she said, "Seeing Rose and Ella together again stirred up all kinds of warm fuzzies you just can't seem to work past."

Jaw clenched, Jackson stayed silent.

"Admission by nonadmission," she said in a sarcastic tone over the soft rock she had pulsing from the stereo. "Works every time."

"Knock it off, Jules. All right, so yes, seeing Ella again last night was tough, but I'm here with you now, aren't I?"

She snorted. "In body, maybe, but I'm afraid your heart's halfway down the block."

"And what if it is? Will you finally admit that the two of us as a couple aren't meant to be?"

"Mom! Dad!" Dillon raced in from the kitchen, out of breath and mud-spattered. "Look what I found!" He held a half-dollar-size box turtle who'd tucked his head and feet into his shell. "Isn't he cool? Can I keep him?"

"I don't know, bud," Jackson said. The last time they'd kept critters, it'd been a death sentence for the half-dozen tadpoles.

"Of course, you can, angel." Julie kissed the top of the boy's head. "Just as soon as you get cleaned up, we'll go to the pet store for a terrarium."

"Thanks, Mom!" Nearly dropping the tiny creature, he squeezed her in a fierce hug. "You're the best!"

Jackson sighed.

"What?" Julie asked.

He relayed the tadpoles' fate, but it didn't phase her.

"It's important that Dillon be responsible for caring for animals." Great, Julie was in hyper-parent mode. "How else do you think he'll learn to be a good father?"

Gee, perhaps by example? But then as of late, Jackson had hardly proven effective in that capacity. Maybe Julie was right? Not only about the damned turtle, but the two of them?

A MONTH PASSED, during which Jackson became fairly adept at going through the motions of life. He worked. Played with Dillon. Helped Julie with meals whenever she was in town. The two things he couldn't manage were making peace with his decision to remarry or forgetting his love for Ella.

He ran into her a lot.

Most recently when dropping off Dillon at a birthday party the twins had also been invited to. Ella had looked amazing, the sound of her laughter as she'd chatted with Ben Matthews's mom at the front door had torn through him. If his decision to stay with Julie was so right, why did it increasingly feel wrong?

Another week passed.

Bringing him seven days closer to sealing his fate.

Two weeks to go until the quiet, courthouse ceremony Julie had planned to renew their vows. After which, she would be commuting back and forth to Kansas City until finding a new job. She'd also talked about starting her own firm, but wasn't yet sure that was what she wanted to do.

Oddly enough, the more determined she was to be a good mom, the more his heart opened to her, only not in the way a man should love his wife. He was remarrying her strictly for Dillon's sake. And the boy couldn't have been more thrilled—well, except for when Julie had given him a puppy. The chocolate lab was lovable and cute, but a royal pain in Jackson's behind, as it seemed he was the one doing most of the puppy parenting.

Jackson shook his head as he waited for *Nosy* to finish sniffing a tree so they could continue their stroll around the neighborhood.

In the still of night, it didn't escape him how happy sounds from happy families danced on the warm air. On the sidewalk, his ears caught snippets of children's laughter floating through open windows, and mothers and fathers reading bedtime stories. He usually went out of his way to bypass Ella's house, but tonight he had to see it.

The boys' bedroom lights were already off, but the living-room lamps were still on, spilling their golden glow onto the porch where Ella sat rocking, staring out at nothing in particular.

She looked beautiful.

He had never wanted her more.

His heart told him he had no business marrying Julie when it was Ella he loved, but because of Dillon, he wasn't sure what else to do.

"I DIDN'T KNOW ELLA'S boys were on Dillon's team." To the first baseball game of the season, Julie had worn a white leather designer pantsuit with red baseball stitching up the pant's side seams and jacket sleeves. Her red leather heels teetered on the park's gravel parking lot.

"Yep," Jackson said, holding his hand out to her to help her into the stands. She was soon to become his wife again. He should've been ecstatic, but all he seemed capable of doing was staring at Ella where she sat twenty feet away in the stands. Wearing jean cutoffs and a red Brown Beavers team shirt and hat, she cheered her boys through their warm-ups, belting out an occasional, "Way to go!"

The physical differences between Julie and Ella were striking. Both were attractive, but Ella's happy-go-lucky, caring spirit shone through her every action and move, showing even in her glowing complexion and the bouncy ponytail stuck through the hole in the back of her cap. He still loved her. Trouble was, he loved his son more. And he hated that—the fact that because of his feelings for Ella, his devotion to his son had become a sort of *trouble*. How had Jackson allowed his life to get to this point?

Ella glanced his way, only to sharply avert her gaze.

Had she felt his stare?

"Hi, Ella!" Julie called out, settling on the same row in the bleachers as their neighbor. "Gorgeous day for baseball, isn't it?"

"Sure is," Ella said, her brittle smile nowhere close to reaching her eyes.

The day was hot and muggy, puffy clouds threatening rain by later that afternoon. Lousy baseball weather. Had that been the best Julie could do in regard to small talk?

"Your…ah…" Jackson cleared his throat before finishing

what he'd started saying to Ella "…boys looked good in batting practice the other day."

"Thanks." Brrr. Despite the day's stifling heat, ice could've formed from Ella's stare. "Dillon looked good, too."

Jackson nodded.

Thankfully, the game started, and Jackson and Ella both focused on their sons.

Julie, meanwhile, alternated between watching the game and talking on her cell.

Parents cheered.

Some yo-yo big brother of the opposing team blared an air horn every time the Polk Possums hit a run.

The guy seated next to Jackson wolfed a chili cheese dog with so many onions it was giving Jackson heartburn just smelling them.

Between the second and third innings, Ella got up to go to the concession stand. A few minutes after she'd made her exit, Jackson said to Julie, "I'm…ah…going to the john. Be right back."

As she was once again chatting, she waved him on his way.

Hustling through the stands, Jackson found Ella at the end of the snack line. "Oh—hey," he said casually, trying to act as if he hadn't been seeking her out.

Arms crossed, she refused to make eye contact.

"Look," he said, "I get it if you don't want anything to do with me, but—"

"It's not that," she said, finally looking his way. "Jackson, I miss you. But now that you're back with Julie, I can't really call you to chat."

"Guess you're right," he said, hands in his pockets, wishing she didn't smell so damned good. Like flowers and cupcakes and maybe even all that chocolate ice cream she so loved. "Sorry."

"You have nothing to be sorry about. You chose the path you felt best for your son. How can I blame you for putting Dillon first?"

"I know, Ell, but—"

She hugged him, killing him with her innate kindness. Leaving him wishing she'd yell, shout or hit. Anything but giving him this unconditional understanding that made him feel worse than ever about having, in a sense, led her on. From the start, she'd wanted to steer clear of him. She'd warned him nothing good could come of their relationship when so much was emotionally at stake with his son. "It's okay," she said, letting him go. "I mean, it's not even a little bit okay…" Eyes big and gorgeous and shining, she added, "but I've come to terms with this—us. Or, I guess that would be the lack thereof. Of us."

Her speech left him hot and cold and aching down deep in his bones. Like he'd caught the flu. But what he had was a thousand times worse, because the pain of losing Ella wasn't leaving in twenty-four measly hours.

ELLA HAD BEEN THROUGH a lot of tough things in her life. Witnessing countless deaths, telling parents their toddlers had cancer. But letting Jackson return to Julie while pasting a smile on her face ranked right up there with the worst.

With the excuse of needing to speak with another baseball mom, after purchasing her diet cola, Ella had retreated to the guest side of the stands to watch the remainder of the game in relative privacy.

While intellectually she got the fact that Jackson was making the right decision—the only decision—he could as a parent, her heart didn't come close to being able to understand. Plain and simple, she loved him. She'd have done anything for him. For his son. Unfortunately for her, the best gift Ella could give Jackson and Dillon was freedom from whatever feelings they'd once shared.

ANOTHER COUPLE OF DAYS passed. Endless hours of Jackson feeling nearly suffocated by his decision to reunite with his ex.

Night after night, he walked the dog.

Hoping, praying for a glimpse of Ella on her porch.

Hoping, praying Ella wouldn't be on her porch. For if she was, would he have the strength to walk by without at least saying hello? Which would be fine if he'd had the willpower to end things there.

Thursday night, stepping deeper into the shadows made by a streetlight and a gangly oak, he made a valiant stab at watching her from afar, but then Nosy began to bay.

Ella stopped rocking to stare out at the street. "Jackson? And is that the new puppy I've been hearing so much about?" Dillon and the twins had made their peace in the way kids seemed able to do, but they didn't seem as close as they'd once been.

Praying still more for strength to get through the next five minutes or so, Jackson forced a smile, then wound his way across the yard to Ella's front porch. "Hey."

Nosy, being true to her name, wriggled and sniffed her way to Ella, who'd risen and now knelt, rubbing the puppy's ears.

"She's adorable," Ella said. "Her name is highly apropos."

"I guess," Jackson said, not in the mood for small talk when just being near Ella made him feel as if his entire world were being torn apart.

"You all right?" she asked in that gentle manner of hers, always caring more about others than herself.

"As good as can be expected," he said.

"I'm sorry we didn't get a chance to talk at the boys' last game."

"It's all right."

"I guess I'm still getting used to seeing you with Julie."

"Really," he said, "I wouldn't blame you for never wanting to talk to me again."

For the longest time, she looked at her feet. What was she thinking? Why was he suddenly consumed with needing to know?

"The, um, few times Dillon has been over for a visit," she said, unhooking the puppy's leash so she could lift her for closer inspection, "he's seemed elated. About you and Julie."

"He is."

"And you?" Jackson was shocked that after all he'd put her through, she'd even care. Nosy licked her chin, and Ella laughed. "She has puppy breath."

How he'd missed Ella's laugh, her smile, her kisses….

"I'm sure you've heard through the grapevine about Rose having settled in with the Donaldsons?" Ella switched subjects.

Not trusting himself to speak past the gnawing lump in his throat, he nodded.

"It killed me to give her up, but I'm slowly coming around. I visit her a lot, and watch her for Claire whenever she needs a sitter."

"That's nice."

"Speaking of nice," she said, talking more to the puppy than to him, in a playful tone she'd often used with the baby. "I got quite a shocker when at the last city board meeting your father strolled up to apologize for essentially kicking me out of his party. He confessed his sciatica had been acting up, and that he hadn't been feeling good."

Was it wrong of Jackson to wonder how that explained Walter's grumpy behavior for the last twenty years?

"You'll be pleased to know that for the moment anyway, I seem to have conquered my ice cream habit. I've even lost three whole pounds." Grinning, she did one of those high-fashion spins, and that was it. He lost it.

"I—I can't do this," Jackson said, reaching for the damned dog.

"Do what?" she asked.

"Stand here, acting as if we're just casual friends when with every fiber of my being, I want *you* to be my wife—not Julie. I want to laugh with you and go to our kids' bingo and baseball games with you and eat ice cream with you till we both gain twenty pounds. I miss you, Ell…" Unmanly tears threatening to spill, he turned his back to her.

"I miss you, too," she said softly from behind him. He caught a whiff of her light floral perfume and that was his final undoing.

"I can't go on living this lie," he admitted, turning to face her. "You once told me I need to be the parent, and that I can't let Dillon make the decisions for how to run our lives, but in agreeing to remarry Julie, that's exactly what I've done. How long will it be till she grows bored with us? Everything in me tells me her being infatuated with Dillon is only a temporary thing. When she takes off again, who's going to be here to pick up the pieces? Me and you, Ell, that's who. Only how much better would it be for my boy if we were already a family when Julie's news comes?"

"Wh-what are you saying?" Ella asked, nuzzling the puppy's head as she once had Rose's. The woman was a natural-born mother. One Jackson very much wanted to help him raise his son.

"I'm saying I love you." Choppy tears came, but he didn't

care. The sense of freedom bursting through him at having shed this awful burden was too great to contain. "I can't marry Julie. No matter how badly Dillon wants this, I can't be a good father to him and keep living a lie. In the short run, he's going to hate me, but in the long run, he'll realize me marrying you is for the best."

Ella cleared her throat. "Aren't you forgetting one big part of this newfound plan?"

"What's that?"

"Asking me if I even care to be a part of it?"

"Well?" Easing his hands around her waist felt akin to coming home. "Do you?"

Ella knew the smart thing would be saying no, but when it came to matters of the heart, she'd always let her emotions lead. At the moment, her every instinct screamed to pick up where she'd left off with this wonderful man. Yes, he'd made some mistakes, but hadn't they all?

They'd take things slow.

Handle Dillon and her boys with kid gloves.

In time, they would all come around.

"You're killing me here," Jackson said, giving her a squeeze. "Are you on board with my plan?"

"Since you put it so eloquently," she said, with her free hand tracing the outline of his brow, his cheek, his dear lips, "yes, Jackson Tate, I will give you a second chance. But only under one condition."

"Name it."

She handed the whining puppy off to him. "You get to potty train the newest member of our family."

Epilogue

"Who wants lemonade?" Ella asked, one hand on the sweating pitcher and the other on her active tummy. Judging by the kicking, her baby was a soccer fan.

"Meee!" Dillon cried, squirming on the picnic table bench.

"Me, too!" Oliver said, trying to out-shout his stepbrother. Though a year had passed since she and Jackson had made their relationship official with a romantic backyard wedding, her eldest and Dillon were still vying for who was going to be King of the Mountain. So far, Oliver seemed to be in the lead, but every so often, Dillon gave him a run for his money when it came to out-eating him or defeating video-game monsters. For the most part, though, they'd become best friends, for which Ella was thankful.

"Owen?" After filling the two boys' glasses, Ella glanced his way. "Want some?"

"No, thank you."

"You feeling all right?" Jackson asked Owen while scooping potato salad onto each of the boys' plates. His parents were across the yard, chatting with his brother and Julie in front of the new water garden. On his off days, Jackson had transformed Ella's once-drab backyard into a wonderland fit for their nuptials. Julie had surprised them all by remaining true to her word in staying close to Dillon. She'd moved back into the home she'd once shared with Jackson, and now kept Dillon with her most every weekend. Weekdays, she worked hard at the law practice she'd set up downtown. Walter had gradually thawed to the point that he'd actually asked Ella's opinion in the design of his dealership's new digs.

Owen shrugged.

"What's wrong?" Ella asked.

He nodded toward Oliver and Dillon. "They're always together, and no one plays with me anymore."

"Honey," Ella crooned, perching next to him on the end of the bench, "of course they still play with you."

"Uh-uh."

"Tell you what," she said, "when your baby sister gets here, you can be her best friend."

"But that won't be the same."

"I know, honey, but don't you think she'll need a best friend and a big brother?"

"I guess," he said, chin dragging to his chest.

"Poor little guy," Jackson whispered to her when they were both back at the grill. As usual, Ella was starving and the scent of grilling burgers had her stomach growling and kicking. "Think we should let him invite one of his friends from school over?"

Ella kissed her husband. "I'm so glad I married a smartypants. I'll go call Billy from down the street."

"Come here, Nosy," Owen said to the family dog who'd grown from a puppy into a mini-moose. "You're the only one who loves me."

Ella and Jackson shared a look.

He took her hand in his for a moment, intertwining their

fingers. Reminding her with no more than a touch that with this latest child-rearing crisis, she was no longer on her own, but part of a team. A wonderfully hectic, crazy, happy team she never ceased being thrilled to be part of.

"I love you," he mouthed.

"Love you, too."

And she did. Lord, how she did.

* * * * *

THOROUGHBRED LEGACY
*The stakes are high when it comes to love,
horse racing, family secrets
and broken promises.*

*A new exciting Harlequin continuity series coming soon!
Led by* New York Times *bestselling author Elizabeth Bevarly*
FLIRTING WITH TROUBLE

Here's a preview!

THE DOOR CLOSED behind them, throwing them into darkness and leaving them utterly alone. And the next thing Daniel knew, he heard himself saying, "Marnie, I'm sorry about the way things turned out in Del Mar."

She said nothing at first, only strode across the room and stared out the window beside him. Although he couldn't see her well in the darkness—he still hadn't switched on a light…but then, neither had she—he imagined her expression was a little preoccupied, a little anxious, a little confused.

Finally, very softly, she said, "Are you?"

He nodded, then, worried she wouldn't be able to see the gesture, added, "Yeah. I am. I should have said goodbye to you."

"Yes, you should have."

Actually, he thought, there were a lot of things he should have done in Del Mar. He'd had *a lot* riding on the Pacific Classic, and even more on his entry, Little Joe, but after meeting Marnie, the Pacific Classic had been the last thing on Daniel's mind. His loss at Del Mar had pretty much ended his career before it had even begun, and he'd had to start all over again, rebuilding from nothing.

He simply had not then and did not now have room in his life for a woman as potent as Marnie Roberts. He was a horseman first and foremost. From the time he was a schoolboy, he'd known what he wanted to do with his life—be the best possible trainer he could be.

He had to make sure Marnie understood—and he understood, too—why things had ended the way they had eight years ago. He just wished he could find the words to do that. Hell, he wished he could find the *thoughts* to do that.

"You made me forget things, Marnie, things that I really needed to remember. And that scared the hell out of me. Little Joe should have won the Classic. He was by far the best horse entered in that race. But I didn't give him the attention he needed and deserved that week, because all I could think about was you. Hell, when I woke up that morning all I wanted to do was lie there and look at you, and then wake you up and make love to you again. If I hadn't left when I did— the way I did—I might still be lying there in that bed with you, thinking about nothing else."

"And would that be so terrible?" she asked.

"Of course not," he told her. "But that wasn't why I was in Del Mar," he repeated. "I was in Del Mar to win a race. That was my job. And my work was the most important thing to me."

She said nothing for a moment, only studied his face in the darkness as if looking for the answer to a very important question. Finally she asked, "And what's the most important thing to you now, Daniel?"

Wasn't the answer to that obvious? "My work," he answered automatically.

She nodded slowly. "Of course," she said softly. "That is, after all, what you do best."

Her comment, too, puzzled him. She made it sound as if being good at what he did was a bad thing.

She bit her lip thoughtfully, her eyes fixed on his, glimmering in the scant moonlight that was filtering through the window. And damned if Daniel didn't find himself wanting to pull her into his arms and kiss her. But as much as it might have felt as if no time had passed since Del Mar, there were eight years between now and then. And eight years was a long time in the best of circumstances. For Daniel and Marnie, it was virtually a lifetime.

So Daniel turned and started for the door, then halted. He couldn't just walk away and leave things as they were, unsettled. He'd done that eight years ago and regretted it.

"It *was* good to see you again, Marnie," he said softly. And since he was being honest, he added, "I hope we see each other again."

She didn't say anything in response, only stood silhouetted against the window with her arms wrapped around her in a way that made him wonder whether she was doing it because she was cold, or if she just needed something—someone— to hold on to. In either case, Daniel understood. There was an emptiness clinging to him that he suspected would be there for a long time.

* * * * *

THOROUGHBRED LEGACY
coming soon wherever books are sold!

Thoroughbred Legacy

Launching in June 2008

A dramatic new 12-book continuity that embodies the American Dream.

Meet the Prestons, owners of Quest Stables, a successful horse-racing and breeding empire. But the lives, loves and reputations of this hardworking family are put at risk when a breeding scandal unfolds.

Flirting with Trouble

by *New York Times* bestselling author

ELIZABETH BEVARLY

Eight years ago, publicist Marnie Roberts spent seven days of bliss with Australian horse trainer Daniel Whittleson. But just as quickly, he disappeared. Now Marnie is heading to Australia to finally confront the man she's never been able to forget.

The stakes are high when it comes to love, horse racing, family secrets and broken promises.

A new exciting Harlequin continuity series coming soon!

www.eHarlequin.com

HT38984R

REQUEST YOUR FREE BOOKS!

2 FREE NOVELS PLUS 2
FREE GIFTS!

Heart, Home & Happiness!

HAR08

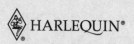